DEFYING DRAKON

BY
CAROLE MORTIMER

First published in Great Britain 2012
by Mills & Boon, an imprint of Harlequin (UK) Limited,
Harlequin (UK) Limited, Eton House, 18-24 Paradise Road,
Richmond, Surrey TW9 1SR

MILLS
BOON

Carole Mortimer was born in England, the youngest of three children. She began writing in 1978, and has now written over one hundred and fifty books for Harlequin Mills & Boon®. Carole has six sons: Matthew, Joshua, Timothy, Michael, David and Peter. She says, 'I'm happily married to Peter senior; we're best friends as well as lovers, which is probably the best recipe for a successful relationship. We live in a lovely part of England.'

Recent titles by the same author:

THE TALK OF HOLLYWOOD
SURRENDER TO THE PAST
TAMING THE LAST ST CLAIRE
  (The Scandalous St Claires)

Did you know these are also available as eBooks?
Visit www.millsandboon.co.uk

My family. You know who you are!

CHAPTER ONE

'Who is she?' Markos asked.

Drakon had telephoned down to his cousin Markos's office just a few minutes ago, and was now in one of the many rooms of the penthouse apartment on the thirtieth floor of the Lyonedes Tower building in Central London, where Drakon stayed whenever he was visiting from the company's New York offices. Markos, naturally, preferred to live away from the building where he worked every day.

Drakon's full attention was focused speculatively on one of several security monitors in front of him as he watched the young woman on the monochrome screen pacing restlessly up and down the room she had been escorted to several minutes ago by Max Stanford, his Head of Security, after causing something of a disturbance in the reception area situated on the ground floor of the building.

She was a tall and willowy young woman, the dark blouse she wore—possibly black or brown—clinging to the outline of small pert breasts, while slim-fitting low-rider jeans revealed a tantalising glimpse of the flatness of her abdomen before curving lovingly over her bottom and the length of her legs. She was probably aged somewhere in her mid to late twenties, with just below shoulder-length straight hair—blonde? Her face was arrestingly beautiful: delicately heart-shaped and dominated by light-coloured eyes. Damn this black and white screen! She had a small straight nose and sensuously full lips.

He glanced at Markos as his cousin came to stand beside him. The family resemblance and their Greek nationality were more than obvious in their harshly sculptured olive-skinned features. Both men were dark-haired and over six feet tall, although at thirty-four Markos was two years Drakon's junior.

'I'm not sure,' Drakon answered. 'Max telephoned a few minutes ago and asked me what I wished him to do with her,' he continued. 'Apparently when he removed her from Reception she refused to tell him anything other than that her name is Bartholomew and she has no intention of leaving the building until she has spoken either to you or me—but preferably me,' he added dryly.

Markos's eyes widened. 'Any relation to Miles Bartholomew, do you think?'

'Could be his daughter.' Drakon had met Miles Bartholomew several times before the other man's death in a car crash six months ago, and there was a definite facial resemblance between him and the young woman they could see on the screen now. Although at sixty-two Miles's hair had been silver, and his tall frame wiry rather than willowy and graceful.

'What do you suppose she wants?' Markos prompted curiously.

Drakon's dark eyes narrowed on the impatiently pacing woman, his mouth thinning to an uncompromising line. 'I have absolutely no idea. But I have every intention of finding out.'

Markos's brows rose. 'You intend talking to her yourself?'

Drakon gave a humourless smile at his cousin's obvious surprise. 'I have asked Max to bring her to me here in ten minutes' time. It is to be hoped she will not have worn a hole in a very expensive carpet before then.'

Markos looked thoughtful. 'Are you sure that's a good idea with our current connection to Bartholomew's young and beautiful widow?'

Drakon deliberately turned his back on the screen. 'Max's alternative was to have her arrested for trespassing and/or disturbing the peace. A move at best guaranteed to bring unnecessary and unwanted publicity to Lyonedes Enterprises,' he said, 'and at worst to have an adverse effect on our relationship with Angela Bartholomew.'

'True,' his cousin conceded. 'But isn't it setting something of a precedent to give in to this type of emotional blackmail?'

Drakon arched arrogant dark brows. 'You are expecting there to be more than one determined young woman in London at the moment who feels the need to stage a sit-in in the reception area of Lyonedes Enterprises until she has been allowed to talk to the company's president?'

Markos gave a rueful shake of his head. 'You've only been in England for two days—hardly long enough for you to have broken any female hearts as yet.'

Drakon's expression remained impassive. 'If, as you say, hearts have been broken in the past, then it has not been my doing; I have never made any secret of the fact that I have no interest in marrying at this time.'

'If ever!' His cousin snorted.

Drakon shrugged. 'No doubt there will come a time when an heir becomes necessary.'

'Just not yet?'

His mouth thinned. 'No.'

Markos eyed him teasingly. 'Miss Bartholomew seems to have piqued your interest...'

There were only two people in the world who would dare to speak to Drakon in this familiar way: his cousin and his widowed mother.

The two men had grown up together in the family home in Athens. Markos had come to live with his aunt and uncle and slightly older cousin after his parents were killed in a plane crash when he was eight years old. It was that closeness, and the fact that they were related by blood, which allowed the younger man certain freedoms of expression where Drakon was concerned. If anyone else but Markos had dared to make a comment on or question Drakon's private life like that, he would very quickly have found himself on the other side of the door. After being suitably and icily chastened, of course.

'I am...curious as to her reasons for coming here,' he acknowledged slowly.

His cousin glanced towards the screen. 'She's certainly beautiful...'

'Yes, she is,' Drakon acknowledged tersely.

Markos shot him another sideways glance. 'Maybe I could sit in on the meeting?'

'I think not, Markos,' he dismissed with dry humour. 'Whatever Miss Bartholomew wishes to talk to me about, she has gone about it in a very unorthodox manner. I do not think the Vice-Chairman of Lyonedes Enterprises showing an admiring interest in her is going to suitably convey our displeasure at her behaviour!'

Markos gave an unrepentant grin. 'Do you have to spoil *all* my fun?'

Drakon smiled in acknowledgement of his cousin's roguish reputation with the ladies even as he glanced down at the plain gold watch secured about his wrist. 'Thompson should be arriving shortly for his ten o'clock appointment. I will join the two of you in your office in ten minutes.'

The other man arched teasing brows. 'Are you sure that will be long enough with the lovely Miss Bartholomew?'

'Oh, yes.' He nodded.

Drakon gave one last glance at the young woman on the screen before striding through to the sitting room of the spacious apartment to stand in front of one of the huge picture windows that looked out over the London morning skyline, hearing his cousin leaving the penthouse a few seconds later as his own brooding thoughts continued to dwell on the impudent Miss Bartholomew.

He had taken over as head of the Lyonedes family business empire on the death of his father ten years ago, and now, aged thirty-six, Drakon knew he was rarely surprised by anything anyone did or said—and was certainly never intimidated by their actions. He was the one whose very presence invariably intimidated others; never the other way about.

And whatever reason Miss Bartholomew felt she had for her unacceptable behaviour, she would very shortly be made aware of that fact…

Gemini stopped pacing and turned to frown at the middle-aged man who had earlier introduced himself only as Head of Security for Lyonedes Enterprises as he finally returned to the elegantly furnished room he had made her prison fifteen minutes ago, before abandoning her there and locking the door behind him as he left.

No doubt he had gone off to take instruction from Markos Lyonedes as to what was the best thing to do with her—or maybe he hadn't bothered with that and had just telephoned the police to have her arrested! She doubted the visiting totally elusive Drakon Lyonedes, President of Lyonedes Enterprises, would even be informed of something so trivial as a young woman refusing to leave the building until she was allowed to speak to him.

Gemini had every reason to know just how elusive he was. She had desperately tried repeatedly to make an appointment to speak to the man since she'd learnt of his arrival in England two days ago. But as she had remained stubbornly unwilling to give her reasons as to why she wanted the appointment, her request had been politely but firmly refused by Markos Lyonedes's secretary.

Oh, she had been invited to send in her C.V. to the personnel manager—as if she would ever want to work for a circling shark like Drakon Lyonedes!—but had been refused an appointment with him *or* his cousin, who was Vice-Chairman of the company in charge of the London-based offices. Leaving her with no alternative, Gemini had finally decided determinedly, than to stage a sit-in in the ground floor reception area of Lyonedes Tower.

Only to be firmly removed within minutes of her arrival and locked in a room pending dispatch!

'Let's go.' The tough-looking Head of Security, dressed all in black, his grey hair shaved to a crewcut, stepped back in order to allow her to precede him out of the room. He was probably ex-military.

'I expected handcuffs at the very least!' she drawled as she strolled past him into the marble hallway.

He arched iron-grey brows. 'What exactly did you have in mind?'

Was that amusement she saw in those hard blue eyes? No, surely not! 'Nothing like that, I assure you,' Gemini said dryly.

'That's what I thought.' He nodded as he took a vice-like grip of her arm. 'And handcuffs wouldn't look good in front of the other visitors.'

That remark might have been funny if the man hadn't looked so deadly serious when he made it! 'Where are you taking me?' she prompted with a frown, having tried to resist that steely hold and only succeeded in bruising her arm as the now grim-faced man all but frogmarched her down a long and silent hallway towards the back of the building. 'I asked—'

'I heard you.' He came to a halt beside a lift before deftly punching a security code into the lit keypad.

He'd heard her, but obviously had no intention of satisfying her curiosity. 'I'm sure this building is far too modern to have a dungeon,' she commented.

'But it does have a basement.' He shot her a narrow-eyed glance as the lift doors opened, and he pulled her in beside him before pressing one of the buttons.

The movement was made altogether too fast for Gemini to be able to see which button he had pressed before the doors closed behind them and the lift began to move. Down? Or up? Whichever it was, the lift was moving so fast her stomach seemed literally to somersault! Or maybe that was just her slightly shredded nerves? She hadn't particularly enjoyed coming to Lyonedes Tower this morning and making such a nuisance of herself, and the dangerous-looking man standing so still and silent beside her certainly didn't inspire confidence as to her future wellbeing!

Maybe trying to force a meeting between herself and either Markos or Drakon Lyonedes hadn't been such a good idea after all?

It had seemed perfectly logical and straightforward when Gemini had considered her options earlier that morning, as she sat in the kitchen of her apartment. But here and now, on her way to goodness' knew where, with a hatchet-faced man who looked as if he was more than capable of killing with his bare hands, it seemed far less so.

It was all Drakon Lyonedes's fault, of course. If the man didn't make it so impossible for people to see or speak with him then there would be no reason for her to resort to such drastic measures as she had this morning. As it was…

Her chin rose defensively as she chanced a glance at the grimly silent man standing beside her. 'Kidnapping is a serious offence, you know.'

'So is making a public nuisance of yourself,' he came back remorselessly.

'Lyonedes Tower isn't exactly public!'

'Keep telling yourself that, love.' Once again she thought she caught a glimpse of humour in those steely blue eyes, before it quickly dissipated and only the steel remained.

'There's nowhere for me to escape to, stuck in this lift, so it's probably safe to let go of my arm now—' She broke off abruptly as the lift came to a gliding halt and the doors slid silently open in front of her.

Not into a basement. Or a dungeon. But into the unlikeliest-looking office Gemini had ever seen…

Probably because it *wasn't* an office, she realised

as Mr Grim pulled her with him into a huge and elegant sitting room. The thick-pile carpet beneath her booted feet was a rich cream colour, and several brown leather armchairs and a huge matching L-shaped sofa were placed near the marble fireplace. Occasional tables bore vases of cream roses, and a matching cream piano stood in one corner of the room, a bar area in another. She easily recognised some of the numerous paintings on the cream walls as being priceless works of art by long-dead artists, and the floor-to-ceiling windows that made up the wall directly in front of her displayed an amazing view of the London skyline.

So—definitely not the basement, then!

'I will ring you when it is time for Miss Bartholomew to leave, Max.'

'Sir.'

Gemini only vaguely registered the Head of Security as he stepped silently back into the lift and departed. She turned sharply to locate the owner of that deep and authoritative voice, her eyes widening in shock as she saw the man silhouetted in front of a second wall of windows, instantly knowing she was looking at the tall, powerful, olive-skinned Drakon Lyonedes himself.

It was perfectly obvious that he was far from pleased. The expression on his handsome face was even grimmer than the one on his Head of Security's.

Drakon Lyonedes was over six feet tall, with wide shoulders, a powerful chest, and long legs clearly defined in a tailored and obviously expensive charcoal-grey suit worn over a white silk shirt and pale grey tie. His dark hair was cut ruthlessly short, and piercing coal-black eyes were set in a face that looked as if it had been hewn from granite. None of the rare photographs of Drakon Lyonedes that had very occasionally appeared in the newspapers over the years had even begun to scratch the surface of the aura of power that surrounded him like an invisible cloak.

Not just power, Gemini realised as an icy shiver ran the length of her spine, but danger—like that of a deadly predator waiting to pounce on its prey.

A powerful and deadly predator who now had *her* firmly fixed in his sights!

Drakon's expression remained unreadable as he took in the colour version of the determined Miss Bartholomew. The straight, shoulder-length hair he had thought might be a pale blonde was in fact an unusual white-gold—the same colour as the long stretches of sandy beach that surrounded his private island off the coast of Greece. Her complexion was the palest ivory, and a perfect background for her eyes, which he could now see were the same deep aquamarine colour as the warm Aegean Sea, and shielded by thick dark lashes. Her full and sensuous lips were an unglossed and natural rose.

In fact she did not appear to be wearing any makeup at all, which was most unusual in his experience…

'Mr Lyonedes, I presume?' she enquired softly, moving with a natural grace as she stepped further into the private sitting room of the penthouse apartment.

'Miss Bartholomew.' Drakon remained unsmiling in response to what had obviously been an attempt at humour on her part. 'Max informs me that you have been most…insistent in your desire to speak with me.'

'Does he?' She continued to stare at him with those aquamarine eyes.

'Sitting on the floor of the reception area and refusing to move till you had either spoken to myself or my cousin *would* appear to be an act of determination, yes,' he pointed out.

'Oh, yes. That.' Gemini grimaced as she tried to gather her scrambled thoughts together—a situation she readily admitted had been brought about by this man's totally overpowering presence! 'Max soon took care of that for you, though,' she said, remembering the ease with which the security man had placed his hands beneath her elbows and just lifted her up from the floor and out of the reception area to that secure room.

Dark brows rose. 'You are on a first-name basis with my Head of Security?'

'I think it's fair to say I'm on an *only* name basis with him—he didn't introduce himself to me earlier, so I know him by the name you just called him.' She shrugged. 'And I wouldn't have needed to be quite so determined if you'd made yourself more accessible,' she said lightly. After all, she could afford to be a little more amenable now that she was actually in the presence of the man himself.

'And why would I wish to do that?' He seemed genuinely baffled by her statement.

'Because— Oh, never mind.' Gemini gave a dismissive shake of her head.

Drakon noticed how the movement caused that cascade of white-gold hair to be caught in the sun's rays, and found himself wondering if the colour was natural or from a bottle. Only to add an inner admonishment for allowing even that small personal interest to creep into this meeting. 'You do realise that causing a nuisance of yourself on private property is—'

'A serious offence,' she finished heavily. 'Yes, your Head of Security has already made it more than clear that you would have been quite within your rights to call the police and have me arrested rather than agree to see me.'

Drakon gave a hard and humourless smile. 'Oh, believe me, that possibility has not yet been dismissed.'

'Oh.' Uncertainty briefly flickered in her eyes as she drew herself up to her full height of possibly five feet ten inches in the two-inch-heeled boots she was wearing. The shirt that fitted so flatteringly over her breasts and the flatness of her abdomen was black in colour, the jeans that clung to that enticingly curvaceous bottom a light blue. 'I only did what I did because I so badly needed to talk to you—'

'Would you care for coffee?'

She blinked. 'What?'

'Coffee?' Drakon indicated the bar area, where a full pot of coffee had been brought up to him earlier and left on the black marble surface along with several black mugs.

'Is it decaf?'

He raised dark brows. 'I think possibly Brazilian, as that is my preferred blend...'

'Then, no, thank you,' she refused politely. 'Unless it's decaffeinated most coffees give me a migraine.'

'Would you like me to send down for some that *is* decaffeinated?'

'No, really. I'm fine.' She smiled.

Drakon had absolutely no idea why he had even made the offer; the sooner the two of them talked and she departed, the better! 'You do not mind if I do?' He didn't wait for her reply before walking over to the bar and pouring a cup of the steaming and aromatic brew, lifting the unsweetened liquid to his lips and slowly taking a sip as he used the respite in conversation to study her over the rim of the mug.

If, as he thought, this young woman *was* the daughter of Miles Bartholomew and the stepdaughter of Angela Bartholomew, then she did not appear or behave at all as one might have expected of the only child of a multimillionaire industrialist. Her clothing was as casual as that of any of the dozens of young women Drakon had seen as he was driven from the airport into central London two days ago, her unusually coloured hair was styled simply in straight layers and—as he had already noted—the fragile loveliness of her face appeared bare of make-up. Her fingernails were short and unvarnished on long and elegant hands, and she raised one to flick a wayward strand of that long white-gold hair over her shoulder.

The appearance of Miles Bartholomew's daughter—if this was she—was indeed unexpected. Her familiar manner towards Drakon—with a complete lack of the awe with which he was usually treated!—was even more so…

He placed the black mug carefully back on the bar beside him before walking softly, unhurriedly, across the room until he stood only inches away from her. Their gazes were almost on a level as she stood only three or four inches shorter than his own six feet and two inches in height.

'We appear to have omitted to introduce ourselves. As you have already guessed, I am Drakon Lyonedes. And you are…?'

'Gemini,' she blurted out. 'Er—Gemini Bartholomew. I'm Miles Bartholomew's daughter.' She thrust out a hand, her cheeks having become coloured the same beguiling rose as the fullness of her lips.

Gemini…

Drakon inwardly appreciated how well that name

suited her as he took the slenderness of her hand in his
much larger one. The name was as unusual and beautiful as this young woman was herself...

'And what is it you believe that only I can do for you,
Miss Bartholomew?'

Gemini felt a quiver of awareness travel the length
of her spine as Drakon Lyonedes continued to hold her
hand captive in his much stronger one. His skin was
cool to the touch, but at the same time the huskiness
of his voice seemed to wash over her senses with the
warmth of a lingering caress.

Surely she must have imagined that *double entendre*
in his question?

Even the thought that she might not have done was
enough to make her aware of the fact that not only
was she not prepared for the sheer physical presence of
the head of Lyonedes Enterprises, but she hadn't even
begun to guess—couldn't possibly have imagined!—
the rawness of the overwhelming sexuality he exuded.

It was a raw sexuality Gemini would have preferred
not to have even recognised, let alone responded to,
when she had every reason to suspect that he was currently involved in an affair with the stepmother she disliked so intensely...

CHAPTER TWO

JUST the thought of her stepmother was enough to make Gemini pull her hand abruptly from Drakon's—no doubt his hand had touched the detested Angela in ways Gemini didn't even want to begin to imagine!

With an inward shudder she thrust her hand firmly behind her back before taking a determined step away from him. 'There's only one thing you can do for me, Mr Lyonedes,' she assured him flatly. 'And that is to withdraw the offer you've made to purchase Bartholomew House from my father's widow!'

Drakon studied Gemini Bartholomew from beneath narrowed lids, noting the wings of colour that had appeared in those ivory cheeks, and the over-bright glitter of emotion now visible in her beautiful sea-green eyes as she glared at him. 'And why, when the sale is due to be completed in only two weeks' time, would you imagine I might wish to do that, Miss Bartholomew?' he said slowly.

A pained frown appeared between those long-lashed aquamarine eyes. 'Because it isn't hers to sell, of course. To you or anyone else!'

'I believe my legal department have checked all the necessary paperwork and are completely satisfied with their results,' Drakon assured her smoothly, no longer completely sure what or who he was dealing with. He certainly had no one else's word but hers that she was who she claimed to be.

From all accounts her behaviour had been less than rational ever since she'd entered the building, and the claim she had just made, along with that slightly wild glitter in those stunning Aegean-coloured eyes, would seem to imply a certain wobble in her emotional balance. Perhaps, after all, he should have heeded Markos's advice and not agreed to meet privately with this unusual young woman?

'I'm sure that they were.' She now gave an impatient shake of that white-gold head. 'When I said Bartholomew House wasn't Angela's to sell, I meant morally rather than legally.'

The tension in Drakon's shoulders relaxed slightly. 'I see,' he murmured.

Somehow Gemini doubted that!

And she didn't care for the way in which Drakon was now regarding her so sceptically with those piercing coal-black eyes of his from between narrowed lids.

No doubt he already thought she was slightly deranged after her behaviour in the reception area, without her now claiming that Bartholomew House wasn't Angela's to sell, and then admitting that it was! Except it wasn't. How could it be, when Bartholomew House in London had been owned by a Bartholomew since—well, for ever? And Angela wasn't really a Bartholomew. The other woman had been the second wife of Gemini's father, and only married to him for three years before his death six months ago—how could Angela possibly begin to understand the sense of tradition, of belonging, that a Bartholomew living in Bartholomew House had given to her family for hundreds of years?

As Gemini knew only too well, it wasn't a question of her stepmother not understanding those things; Angela didn't *want* to understand them, and had made it more than clear these past few months that as she was Miles's widow the house was legally hers. As such, she could do whatever she wanted with it. And if that involved selling Bartholomew House to Lyonedes Enterprises, to the powerful, mega-wealthy man she had implied was her lover, then that was exactly what Angela intended to do!

Gemini scowled her complete frustration with the situation. 'I realise that you and Angela are…involved, but—'

'I beg your pardon?' Drakon raised an arrogant dark brow.

'Oh, don't worry.' She waved a placatory hand at his frowning countenance. 'I don't consider your having a relationship with my stepmother so soon after my father's death as being any of my business.'

'If that's true it's very…magnanimous of you,' Drakon said slowly.

'Oh, it's true,' Gemini assured him—even if, now that she had met him, she couldn't help but wonder how such a powerful and charismatic man could possibly find a woman like Angela attractive.

Her father at least had had the excuse of deep feelings of loneliness after the death of Gemini's mother just a year before he and Angela had been introduced, as well as being deeply flattered by the attentions of a beautiful woman over twenty-five years his junior. But Drakon Lyonedes was as rich as Croesus, for goodness' sake, and as handsome and powerful as any of his Greek gods. As such, he could surely have any woman he wanted. So why would he bother with a mercenary like Angela? There really was no accounting for a man's taste!

'Please continue,' Drakon invited coolly.

'I'm not sure that I should,' she said, suddenly wary.

He shrugged those broad shoulders. 'You obviously disapproved of your father's second marriage…?'

'No, that wasn't it.' Having started this conversation, Gemini now felt uncomfortable revealing too much of her family history to a man she had, after all, only just met. Especially as, if Angela was to be believed, that man was involved with her. 'I just thought perhaps my father should have waited a little longer before remarrying. He was feeling pretty low when he and Angela met—my mother had died the previous year, after thirty years of marriage, and he was desperately lonely.' She shrugged. 'It seemed to me to be a typical on-the-rebound thing.'

'But your father did not agree?'

Gemini winced. 'He had been incredibly unhappy since my mother died, and he seemed so happy with Angela that I just didn't have the heart to voice any of my doubts to him.'

'You loved him very much?'

'Very much,' she confirmed gruffly.

'So he and Angela married despite your misgivings?'

She nodded. 'I just wanted him to be happy again. I'd tried my best to fill the gap that she left, but no matter how close we were it really isn't possible for a daughter to take the place of a life-mate,' she added sadly.

A life-mate…

Having witnessed his own parents' long and happy marriage, Drakon was not unfamiliar with the concept; he had just never heard it described in quite those terms before.

In retrospect, it was a fitting way to describe the closeness that had existed between his own parents—their marriage had been one of friendship and trust as much as love. A love that had encompassed both their 'sons', and which now caused his long-widowed mother to resort to constant lectures on the wonderful state of matrimony whenever he or Markos visited her at her home in Athens and she encouraged at least one of them to marry and give her the grandchildren she so dearly longed for. Unfortunately neither Markos nor Drakon had found a woman they could even contemplate spending the rest of their lives with, let alone be that elusive 'life-mate' Gemini Bartholomew had referred to.

As a child Drakon had just assumed that everyone's parents were as happily married as his own, that their deep love and friendship for each other was the norm. In his teens and twenties, as the Lyonedes heirs, Drakon and Markos had enjoyed dating and bedding a variety of beautiful women, with no thought of falling in love and marrying. It had taken Drakon years to realise that he hadn't felt even the beginnings of love for any of those women—that in fact the type of love his parents had for each other was the exception rather than the norm.

Now, at the age of thirty-six, Drakon believed himself to be too hardened and cynical ever to welcome that emotional vulnerability into his life. Even if he was lucky enough to find it.

'You and your father were close?' he prompted softly.

'Very.' Tears flooded those sea-green eyes.

'I did not mean to upset you—'

'It's okay,' she assured him gruffly. 'I just—I still miss him so much.'

Drakon shifted uncomfortably. 'Are you sure I cannot get you something to drink?'

'No. Really. I'll be fine.' She blinked back those tears as she continued determinedly, 'Things changed between us—became…difficult once Daddy was married to Angela.'

'He was unhappy in the marriage?'

She had already revealed more to this man than she had intended doing; there was absolutely no reason for him to know of the disillusionment that had set in within months of her father's second marriage. 'I'm sure I've already bored you with enough family details for one day, Mr Lyonedes,' she said huskily. 'I've only told you the things I have in an effort to help you to understand the…the awkwardness, of this situation.'

He nodded briskly, obviously accepting her explanation. 'What I fail to understand is what you think I can do about any of it.'

Unfortunately, now that Gemini was confronted with the man himself, she was wondering the same thing! Sitting at home in her apartment, going over the conversation she wanted to have with Drakon Lyonedes, it had all seemed so much simpler than it was in reality. And the fact that the man was so completely and disconcertingly handsome wasn't helping the situation.

Nor was the fact that, in spite of knowing he was intimately involved with the despised Angela, Gemini actually found herself appreciating those tall, dark and dangerous good looks…

How much greater would that appreciation be if she *didn't* know he was involved with Angela? Gemini dreaded to think!

She nervously moistened the dryness of her lips with the tip of her tongue before speaking. 'As I've said, I would like you to withdraw your offer for Bartholomew House.'

'Which, unless I have misunderstood the situation, would not seem to be any of your concern. It was Angela Bartholomew who inherited the house on your father's death and not you,' Drakon pointed out.

'But she shouldn't have done,' Gemini insisted. 'Daddy assured me only weeks before he died that he intended making a new will—one that would clearly state that Bartholomew House was to come to *me* when he died.'

'Something he obviously failed to do before his unexpected death.'

She gave a pained wince. 'Well...yes.'

'He left you nothing?'

Gemini didn't particularly care for the censure she could hear in Drakon's tone. 'I wouldn't call the cherished memories of the love and caring he always had for me nothing!'

That sculptured mouth thinned. 'As I am sure you are well aware, I was talking of what you English refer to as "bricks and mortar".'

'It wasn't necessary. My parents set up a substantial trust fund for me years ago,' she dismissed stiffly. 'But, as I've said, my father assured me that it was his intention to ensure that Bartholomew House came to me after...after his death.'

'Unfortunately we only have your word for that.'

'I am not in the habit of lying, Mr Lyonedes!'

'I was not suggesting that you are.' Drakon sighed his irritation, both with this conversation and his feelings of discomfort at her obvious distress at her father's recent demise and the loss of her family home. 'Only that perhaps you should be discussing all these things with your father's lawyers rather than with me.'

'I already have,' she admitted heavily.

'And...?'

She sighed. 'And they acknowledge that my father informed them only weeks before he died that he was in the process of writing a new will.'

Drakon gaze sharpened. 'But he failed to present this will to them?'

'It would appear so,' she confirmed shakily. 'As such, they agree with you. In the absence of this new will, clearly stating that Bartholomew House was to be separate from all my father's other properties, then Angela is entitled to it as well.'

'It is not a case of my agreeing or disagreeing,' Drakon stated. 'The law is simply the law—no matter what may have been stated verbally. Besides which,' he continued firmly as she would have interrupted, 'if I were to withdraw my own offer for the house and land I have no doubts that your stepmother would simply find another buyer.'

'I realise that—which is why I've come up with another proposal. If you are agreeable, that is?' Those sea-green eyes had brightened excitedly.

Drakon closed his own eyes briefly, before opening them once again to study Gemini from beneath lowered lashes.

From the things she had just revealed to him concerning the Bartholomew family, she was perhaps exactly who she claimed to be. Nevertheless, as she'd come here today with the sole intention of persuading him to stop his company's purchase of Bartholomew House, Drakon somehow doubted this 'proposal' would be any less irregular!

'Of course you would have to agree not to tell Angela anything about it for now,' she added worriedly. 'Otherwise I know she would do everything

in her power to prevent it—to the point of withdraw-
ing from the sale of Bartholomew House to Lyonedes
Enterprises.'

Drakon's mouth thinned. 'Not without incurring a
severe financial penalty for reneging on our present ar-
rangement.'

'That's something, at least,' she breathed shakily.

'Miss Bartholomew—'

'Please call me Gemini,' she invited softly.

'Gemini,' Drakon agreed abruptly, although just
voicing that unusual name seemed to add a level of intimacy to this already unusual situation that he wasn't
sure he felt altogether comfortable with. 'You are obviously under a misapprehension concerning my—' He
broke off as he saw Markos reappear at the top of the
private spiral staircase leading directly from the offices
below.

Gemini frowned as she sensed that his attention was
no longer on her but directed somewhere behind her.
Her breath caught in her throat as she turned and found
herself looking at a dark and handsome man so similar
in looks to Drakon Lyonedes that he surely had to be
related to him. No doubt this was Markos Lyonedes,
Drakon's cousin.

Whoever he was, Gemini dearly wished he had
waited just a few minutes more before making his appearance!

'Sorry to interrupt, Drakon.' The man's deep green
gaze was fixed curiously on Gemini even as he spoke
to his cousin. 'I expected you to join me in my office
some time ago.'

Drakon looked down frowningly at his slender gold
wristwatch, surprised to see that he had been talking
with Gemini for almost half an hour rather than the ten

minutes he had originally thought necessary before dismissing her. Incredible!

'I believe Miss Bartholomew has said what she wished to say…?' He turned to give her a pointed glance.

Instead of taking that as the invitation to leave Drakon intended it to be, she turned and walked gracefully across the room to where Markos stood at the top of the staircase. 'I'm pleased to meet you, Mr Lyonedes.' She smiled warmly as she thrust out her hand.

Markos briefly raised dark and questioning brows in Drakon's direction before turning to take her slender hand in his own. 'I assure you the pleasure is all mine, Miss Bartholomew.' Markos's voice had become dark and smoky.

'Gemini,' she invited lightly.

'Markos,' he returned warmly.

Her smile widened. 'I apologise if I've made your cousin late for an important business meeting.'

'Not at all.' Markos's gaze darkened appreciatively as he continued to hold onto that slender hand and looked down into the pale beauty of her face. 'In Drakon's place I wouldn't have been in any hurry to leave you in order to attend a boring business meeting either.'

Drakon found himself suddenly deeply irritated by the obvious flirtation taking place in front of him, and became even more annoyed as Gemini gave a husky and appreciative laugh before deftly extricating her hand from Markos's. 'I will join you downstairs in a moment, Markos,' he bit out harshly.

His cousin gave him an amused glance. 'I would be more than happy to stay here and keep Gemini company until you return from talking with Bob Thompson.'

Drakon's mouth thinned. 'That will not be necessary.

Miss Bartholomew and I will be meeting for dinner this evening in order to conclude our conversation.'

Wide and startled sea-green eyes turned sharply in his direction. 'We will?'

Drakon bit back his inner frustration, having no idea why he had even made such a statement. Except he had not liked the idea of Markos remaining alone here with Gemini any more than he had appreciated the way in which his cousin had held on to her hand for far longer than was necessary or polite…

Implying what, exactly?

This woman had forced her way into his presence today by making a damned nuisance of herself, before making several surprising statements—including one concerning Drakon's relationship with her stepmother. And as a reward for that unacceptable behaviour he was now inviting her out to *dinner*?

No, he had not invited her out to dinner. He had *told* her the two of them would be having dinner together this evening in order to finish this conversation. Not the same thing at all…

'We will,' Drakon stated flatly. 'I will send a car to Bartholomew House to collect you at seven-thirty this evening.'

'I haven't lived at Bartholomew House for years.' Her nose wrinkled ruefully. 'I'm afraid Angela cornered me several months after she and Daddy were married and asked me to leave,' she explained with a grimace.

Drakon scowled darkly, liking the situation between the two Bartholomew women less and less the more he learnt of it.

Admittedly, as the second wife of Miles Bartholomew, Angela had been perfectly within her rights to ask her stepdaughter to find somewhere else to live—especially as Gemini must have been twenty-four or five at the time—but morally...

But as he had already assured Gemini once today, unfortunately morality often had very little to do with anything!

'Then you will give your current address to the receptionist downstairs when you leave so that the car can be directed there,' he ordered.

'I'll go down to Reception with Gemini,' Markos offered.

Drakon shot his cousin a narrow-eyed glance as he once again sensed Markos's interest in this ethereally beautiful young woman. 'I am sure Miss Bartholomew, having already managed to force herself into my presence today, is more than capable of taking herself down in the lift,' he drawled dismissively, feeling an inner satisfaction as he saw the guilty flush that instantly warmed Gemini's cheeks.

Markos gave an amused smile. 'I'm sure she is too. But wouldn't it be better if one of us were to ensure she has actually left the building?'

The blush deepened in Gemini's cheeks. 'I resent the implication that I'm some sort of criminal who needs escorting from the premises!' she defended irritably.

'Forgive me if I inadvertently gave that impression,' Markos apologised.

She nodded. 'I only behaved in the way that I did earlier because I needed to speak to your cousin on a—a personal matter, and it seemed to be the only way to achieve that.'

Drakon now sensed Markos's speculative green gaze on him, aware that after their earlier conversation his cousin no doubt now believed that 'personal matter' was something totally other than what it actually was.

'Escort the lady downstairs by all means, Markos,' he said as he strolled across the room to join them. 'Until later this evening, Gemini,' he added huskily, before turning to descend the spiral staircase without so much as a backward glance.

'Do I have a smudge of dirt on my nose or something?' Gemini shot a puzzled frown at the man standing beside her in the lift as she sensed his silent appraisal.

'Not at all.' Markos shook his head. 'It's just— Drakon has never mentioned knowing you before today.'

Her brows rose. 'That's probably because he *didn't* know me before today!'

'No?'

'Mr Lyonedes—'

'Markos,' he reminded her smoothly.

Oh, he was a charmer, this one, Gemini acknowledged ruefully—but she had no doubt that there was a will of steel every bit as forceful as his cousin's beneath that outer charm. 'Why don't you just say what you have to say, Markos?' she invited.

He shrugged broad shoulders. 'I am merely curious as to your reason for coming here today.'

Gemini smiled. 'There's really nothing for you to be curious about.'

'No?'

'No,' she stated firmly.

'But I *am* correct in assuming you are Miles Bartholomew's daughter?'

Gemini tensed warily. 'Yes...'

Markos pursed his lips. 'As I thought.'

And he was no doubt thinking a lot of other things if he was aware of his cousin's very personal relationship with Gemini's stepmother!

If Angela were to learn that she was having dinner with Drakon this evening, it would no doubt result in her stepmother throwing one of her temper tantrums. But that was Drakon's problem, not Gemini's; there really was nothing more Angela could do to her that she hadn't already done!

'Well, it's been nice meeting you, Markos.' Gemini's smile was now brightly non-committal, and she stepped out of the lift as soon as the doors opened onto the ground floor. 'I'll be sure and leave my address with the receptionist on my way out.'

Thankfully Markos took that for the dismissal it was meant to be and remained standing inside the private lift. 'I hope you enjoy your dinner with Drakon this evening.' He nodded his farewell, amusement still dancing in those deep green eyes as the lift doors slowly closed.

Whether that amusement was directed at Gemini or his cousin, she wasn't sure…

CHAPTER THREE

'I HAD assumed when you suggested we have dinner together this evening that I would be meeting you at a restaurant.'

Drakon's expression remained unreadable as he stood outside the darkened Lyonedes Tower building and watched Gemini climb out of the back of the silver limousine. The black knee-length dress she wore left her arms and shoulders bare, with a tantalising glimpse of the fullness of her breasts above the scooped neckline, and was a perfect foil for that white-gold hair which fell straight and gleaming about her slender shoulders as she straightened. Blusher added colour to her cheeks this evening, and a pale peach glossed the fullness of her lips. She looked breathtakingly beautiful!

He nodded a curt dismissal of the driver, waiting until the other man had climbed back behind the wheel and driven away before turning back to Gemini. 'You have some objection to us dining here at the apartment?'

Gemini didn't have an objection per se. It just didn't seem exactly...*businesslike* for her to dine with Drakon Lyonedes in the intimacy of that amazing apartment with its magnificent—romantic?—views over London. Even if he *was* once again dressed formally in one of those expensively tailored dark suits—charcoal-grey this time—with another white silk shirt, and a pale blue silk tie meticulously knotted at his throat. That square chin was freshly shaven, and the darkness of his hair appeared slightly damp. As if he had just stood naked beneath the shower—

Imagining Drakon naked in the shower was *so* not a good idea when she was already completely aware of him!

He raised dark brows at her lack of reply. 'This is a business discussion, after all, is it not?'

Well, when he put it like that... 'Of course,' Gemini affirmed gratefully, falling into step beside him as they entered the eerily silent and only semi-illuminated building.

They walked over to the lift, the slender three-inch heels on her strappy sandals sounding over-loud in that unnatural silence. She felt their complete aloneness even more once they had stepped inside the private lift to be whisked silently up to the top floor of the building.

'It really is very good of you to agree to talk to me again so soon.' Gemini rushed into awkward speech in an effort to quell her increasing nervousness as she gripped her slender black evening bag tightly in front of her.

Not that she was normally the nervous type. Far from it. She was usually pretty outgoing. But there was just something so broodingly intense about the man standing beside her...

Drakon gave a tight and humourless smile. 'After your less than orthodox behaviour earlier today, you mean?'

A delicate blush warmed her cheeks. 'Yes.'

He nodded. 'There are certain aspects of our conversation earlier that are...incomplete.'

She blinked up at him. 'There are?'

'Oh, yes,' he said grimly.

Gemini brightened. 'Of course—I hadn't finished telling you about my proposal!'

'That too,' he acknowledged.

Too? What other part of their conversation earlier today had been left 'incomplete'?

Gemini had no more time to dwell on that question as the lift doors opened and Drakon stepped back to allow her to precede him into the sitting room of his apartment. The sitting room seemed much more intimate this evening, illuminated only by four lamps placed about the room, and the glittering London skyline stretched enchantingly in the distance through those floor-to-ceiling windows. A small round table was intimately laid for two in front of one of them, tableware and glasses gleaming, three cream candles in the silver candelabra as yet unlit...

'Would you care for a glass of wine?'

Gemini dragged her gaze away from the intimacy of those place-settings to look across at Drakon as he stood by the bar, his face appearing more harshly brooding in the dimmed lighting. 'I—yes, thank you,' she accepted, placing her bag down on the arm of a chair. 'White, if you have it.'

Drakon smiled slightly to himself as he turned away to open and then pour the wine, sensing Gemini's discomfort as she continued to stand in the middle of the room. 'Was the rest of your day pleasant?' he murmured softly as he crossed the room to hand her one of the two glasses of fruity white wine.

She gave him a startled look as she slowly reached out and took the glass he held out to her. 'Er—busy. As usual.'

'Busy in what way?' Those black eyes studied her over the rim of his glass as he sipped the perfectly chilled wine.

Gemini had hardly expected to be discussing what sort of day she'd had when she next saw Drakon! Almost as if they were out on a real date. Which was utterly ridiculous! Not that she was dating anyone at the moment, her last brief romantic interest having ended months ago, but even so… His relationship with Angela apart, Drakon looked as if he ate up willowy blondes for breakfast, chewed them round for the rest of the morning, and then spat out their bones before enjoying a brunette for lunch!

Although perhaps thinking about Drakon eating her up wasn't the best idea when Gemini now found herself unable to look anywhere but at his sculptured mouth as she imagined how those lips would feel against her skin…

'We're always busy the day before a big wedding.' She rushed into speech in an effort to dismiss those erotic and entirely inappropriate thoughts. 'There's the church to decorate, the bride's bouquet and all the corsages and buttonholes to arrange, then in the morning we'll have to do the top table and twenty others in the reception marquee.' She shrugged. 'I have to be up very early tomorrow too in order to make sure it all gets done well before they return from the wedding at four o'clock.'

Exactly why had she felt the need to add that part? she scolded herself. There was absolutely no way she would still be *here* in the morning!

Drakon looked slightly puzzled. 'I'm afraid I have no idea what you're talking about.'

'Oh. Sorry.' She grimaced before taking a quick sip of her wine.

It was excellent. Of course. A perfectly chilled Pinot Grigio, if she wasn't mistaken. Which she probably wasn't; her father had considered learning to recognise a good wine as an important part of her education.

'Delicious wine.' She nodded her approval before placing the glass down on one of the side tables. Delicious, but definitely lethal for her to drink too much of it when she'd barely had time to draw breath all day let alone eat. Especially as her thoughts had already wandered into what it would feel like to have Drakon's mouth on her!

'I am pleased you approve,' Drakon drawled dryly, even as he wondered about the reason for the blush that had now coloured Gemini's cheeks. 'You were about to explain the reason for your involvement in this "big wedding"?' he reminded her.

She nodded, that white-gold hair gleaming pale and silvery in the lamplight. 'I own and run a florist's shop.'

Drakon scowled. 'I didn't know that…'

Gemini shrugged those slender shoulders. 'There's no reason why you should have done.'

Oh, but there was… As soon as his business meeting this morning had been over Drakon had telephoned down to Max Stanford and asked him to check not only whether Gemini was indeed who she claimed to be, but also into the dynamics of the relationship between Gemini and her stepmother. Perhaps he should have asked Max to put together a more detailed personal dossier on Gemini?

To learn that she had a job at all, let alone owned and ran her own florist's shop, came as something of a surprise to him. Miles Bartholomew had come from old money, and had only added to that wealth during his successful business life; as his only child Gemini would surely have no reason to work. Unless…

His jaw tightened. 'I thought you said you were not left without funds when your father died?'

'I wasn't.' She smiled, revealing small and even white teeth. 'As I said, I have a trust fund. I've owned my shop for five years now—I'm afraid I'm just not the type to sit on my backside looking pretty while I wait for some handsome prince to whisk me off my feet and into marriage,' she declared.

This young woman was ethereally beautiful rather than merely pretty, and Drakon had no doubts that there had been plenty of men during her twenty-seven years who would have wished to 'whisk' her off to somewhere probably a lot less permanent than matrimony. Himself included…?

'And do you enjoy owning and running a florist's shop?' he bit out, annoyed with his own thoughts.

'I love it!' She gave him another bright smile, those sea-green eyes glowing.

'And is your shop successful?'

'Very.' Gemini shot Drakon a mischievous sideways glance. 'And that's not me being egotistical—it just is.'

'Please don't put words into my mouth,' he advised dryly. 'And no business "just is" successful. It takes hard work on the part of someone to make it so.'

She eyed him curiously. 'You sound as if you speak from experience?'

He shrugged. 'My father and uncle were the ones to found Lyonedes Enterprises. My cousin and I have merely continued to add to that success.'

Gemini knew these two powerful men had done so much more than that. Lyonedes Enterprises was now one of the most financially strong and successful companies in the world.

'My father also started and ran his own company,' she said. 'He liquidated it all when he retired at sixty.'

'Because you had no interest in running your father's company? Or because he had no son to continue it?' Drakon prompted curiously.

Her smile faltered slightly. 'Both, probably.'

Was that a note of sadness Drakon could hear in Gemini's voice? Perhaps an underlying wistfulness for having grown up an only child? Having spent much of his life growing up with a boisterous younger cousin, Drakon could not even begin to imagine what that must have been like. His parents' house had always seemed filled to overflowing with the two of them, and also many of their friends.

'Unfortunately my talent always lay with flowers and other things that grow.' She brightened. 'Even as a small child I was obsessed with digging in the garden. To the point that my mother finally persuaded my father to give me my own bed in the garden—no doubt in an effort to stop me from digging up his prize roses!' she added affectionately.

Just her talk of her parents was enough to reveal the deep love that had existed between them and Gemini—making Miles Bartholomew's second marriage, to a woman not so much older than Gemini herself, even more difficult for her?

Drakon made a mental note to himself to thank his mother the next time he saw her for never having put Markos and himself through that same unpleasantness. Not that either of them would have been difficult if Karelia *had* decided to marry again after their father's death; they both loved her far too much to wish her anything but happiness.

'I imagine, as you're the owner of a florist's shop, it must be difficult for a man to send you flowers,' he commented.

'Not at all,' Gemini assured him lightly. 'Yellow roses are my favourites, if you ever feel the—' She broke off abruptly, that delicate blush once again warming her cheeks. 'Sorry. Of course you aren't ever going to want to send me flowers.' She grimaced, before turning away to stroll across to the windows that looked out over the illuminated London skyline. 'This really is a magnificent view.'

Yes, it was. Except Drakon wasn't looking at the London skyline but at Gemini herself.

He didn't believe he had ever met another woman quite like her before. Beautiful, obviously accomplished as she ran a successful shop, and from all accounts a loving and loyal daughter to her father despite the less than harmonious relationship that existed between her and her stepmother. And she now felt such a sense of duty towards the home where she had spent her childhood, which had been in her family for over three hundred years, that she had even risked the possibility of Drakon having her arrested earlier this morning.

'Do you play…?'

He smiled slightly as he saw she was looking across at the piano.

'A little.'

'And do you play well?'

'Passably.' He shrugged.

'I'm sure that if you play even a little you do it very well indeed,' she chided teasingly.

Drakon crossed the room to stand beside her. The

softness of her perfume was an enticing mixture of flowers and beautiful woman. 'Why do you say that?' he prompted.

She smiled widely. 'I don't know you very well, but I already know enough about you to realise you're the type of man who, if he chooses to do something, will never do it "passably" well!' Once again that smile faltered and then disappeared as she seemed to realise exactly what she'd just said. And its obvious sexual implications...

Drakon chuckled huskily as that becoming blush once again coloured the ivory smoothness of her cheeks. 'I will take that as a compliment...'

Gemini wasn't at all comfortable with the sudden intimacy between them—an intimacy she knew *she* was completely responsible for creating with her thoughtless comment!

Was it because she hadn't completely dispelled those earlier images of a naked Drakon Lyonedes emerging from the shower from her mind? Probably. She found it a little difficult to think of him in the abstract at all when he was standing beside her. So hot and immediate. As well as dark and dangerously attractive!

She moistened her lips. 'Perhaps we should just concentrate on our business discussion?'

Those dark eyes narrowed, and his mouth was once again a thin and uncompromising line. 'In that case I believe we must first dispense with your mistaken belief that I am currently involved in a personal relationship with your stepmother.'

Gemini turned, her eyes wide. 'Mistaken...?'

'Certainly.' Drakon frowned. 'I have always made a point of never mixing business with pleasure.'

'But—' She gave a slightly dazed shake of her head. 'I don't understand.'

'It is simple enough, surely?' He raised those arrogant dark brows. 'I have no idea why you should have drawn such a conclusion, but I assure you my only connection to your stepmother is one of business. In the form of my purchase of Bartholomew House,' he added, so that there should be absolutely no doubt as to his meaning.

Gemini stared up at him wordlessly. He looked sincere enough. In fact he looked more than sincere—his handsome face was now visibly showing an expression of extreme distaste at the mere suggestion that he might be involved in an affair with Angela...

But her stepmother had told her—

A lie...?

What possible reason could Angela have had to lie about being involved in an intimate relationship with Drakon?

Knowing the other woman as well as Gemini had come to know Angela since her father had died, she found the answer was suddenly all too obvious.

Gemini had tried so hard to like Angela when her father had first introduced her as the woman he intended to marry. Despite the vast age difference between Angela and Miles. Despite the fact that Gemini had believed her father was rushing too hastily into a second marriage. And in spite of the fact that Angela had given every appearance of being nothing more than a voluptuous blonde beauty attracted to Miles's money rather than the man himself.

Yes, despite all those things Gemini had still tried to like and get along with the older woman. For her father's sake, if for no other reason, because she'd known how much he had wanted his second wife and his daughter to be friends.

Whenever the two women had been in Miles's company that had always appeared to be the case. It had only been when Gemini found herself alone with the other woman that Angela's hostility had become so blatantly obvious, in the form of cutting remarks or long, uncomfortable silences.

It had quickly become obvious to Gemini that, other than Miles, the two women had absolutely nothing in common, and that even that common interest differed greatly in its intent. Angela had wanted and demanded all of Miles's attention for herself. The existence of his twenty-something daughter had been more of an embarrassment than anything else. Whereas Gemini had just wanted to see her father happy again.

Angela asking her to move out of the house once she'd married Miles had certainly been no hardship to Gemini. She had only moved back into Bartholomew House after her mother died so that her father wouldn't be left alone there with only his memories. It had been perfectly natural for her to move out again in order to leave the newly married couple to their privacy.

It was the fact that Angela had made the request without Miles's knowledge and knowing full well that Gemini would never tell him what she had done that had been hard to bear. Angela had made it obvious to Gemini that she resented any time father and daughter spent together—to the point that she'd ensured it rarely happened. It had been an attitude that was never visible whenever Miles was present. Angela's behaviour then had been sickeningly kittenish as she'd continued to wrap her much older and totally smitten husband about her manicured, sexy little finger.

In the circumstances, was it any wonder that Angela had enjoyed implying to Gemini that she had managed to capture the interest of someone like Drakon Lyonedes—a man half Miles's age and probably a dozen times richer?

Knowing Angela as well as she did, Gemini thought the other woman believed it was only a matter of time, anyway, until she made the fabricated affair into a reality. So what did it matter if she'd exaggerated the situation to Gemini now? And if it didn't happen who was ever going to contradict Angela's claims when the man himself was so utterly elusive?

Except Gemini had now met Drakon, and she felt extremely foolish for having believed the other woman's boast about his being infatuated with her. Gemini had no doubt Angela was lying to her; Drakon Lyonedes wasn't the type of man to be infatuated with *any* woman. Besides, being so arrogantly self-assured he obviously never felt the need to lie about any of his actions—least of all his involvement with a woman!

'Am I right in assuming this information was given to you by your stepmother?' he prompted harshly.

Gemini flinched at the disgust underlying his tone. 'Perhaps I misunderstood her.' She gave an uncomfortable lift of her shoulders. 'I— She mentioned how…nice you were.' *Sexily gorgeous* had been her exact words, actually, but Gemini really couldn't bring herself to tell him that! 'Maybe I just let my imagination take that a step further than Angela actually intended—'

'I believe you assured me earlier that you do not lie?' Drakon cut in.

She winced. 'I try not to, no…'

'Then do not do so now,' he advised her coldly.

'I believe I said I might have been mistaken,' she said uncomfortably.

'And do you really believe that?'

'What I believe is that Angela was trying to hurt me by boasting of how quickly she had replaced my father in her bed,' Gemini acknowledged shakily. 'You must have thought I was completely off my head this morning when I started rambling on about the affair you were having with Angela.' She offered him an embarrassed smile.

He gave a derisive snort. 'Not completely, no.'

'You've *never* been intimately involved with Angela, have you?'

'No,' he confirmed.

'Oh, God, I'm so sorry!'

'Here—drink some more of your wine.' Drakon moved to pick up Gemini's glass and handed it to her, inwardly seething at Angela Bartholomew and the lies she had told her stepdaughter. In order to hurt her? No doubt. For himself, Drakon took exception to any woman claiming to have a relationship with him that simply did not, never had and never would exist. Especially in the case of the voluptuous Angela Bartholomew.

Would he resent it quite as much if it had not been the intriguing and beautiful Gemini to whom that lie had been told?

Drakon didn't even want to think about the implications of that question, let alone find an answer for it! 'Not everything your stepmother told you about me was a lie. Lyonedes Enterprises *is* in the process of purchasing Bartholomew House and its grounds from her,' he reminded her softly.

Gemini gave a pained frown. 'I don't understand why

you would even want to own a big house and grounds in London when you have this wonderful apartment to stay in whenever you're in England.'

Drakon drew in a sharp breath even as he stepped slightly away from her. 'It is not my intention ever to live in Bartholomew House.'

She looked puzzled. 'It isn't?'

'No.'

'Then who is—? Perhaps I shouldn't ask that.' She shot him an awkward look. 'Obviously you have your reasons for wanting to own a house in London.'

Drakon's eyes narrowed at Gemini's more than obvious assumption that those reasons probably involved a woman. 'I believe I stated that Lyonedes Enterprises is in the process of completing the purchase of Bartholomew House?' he reiterated firmly.

She frowned. 'What does that mean, exactly?'

His jaw tightened. 'Precisely what I said.'

She gave a confused shake of her head. 'Are you going to open up more offices there, or something?'

Drakon's mouth firmed as he sensed impending disaster. 'Or something.'

Gemini looked at him searchingly, but as usual that dark and harshly handsome face revealed none of his inner thoughts or emotions. This man could have posed for the original Egyptian Sphinx, his expression was so damned inscrutable!

She swallowed before speaking. 'Exactly *what* are you, as President of Lyonedes Enterprises, intending to do with Bartholomew House?' She ensured the preciseness of her question didn't allow for further prevarication on his part.

'Perhaps we should have dinner first—'

'Is that because you're hungry? Or because I probably won't want to eat once you've answered my question?' Gemini prompted shrewdly.

'The latter,' he allowed grimly.

Her chin rose determinedly. 'Drakon, will you please tell me what your intentions are with regard to Bartholomew House?'

He breathed deeply. 'For the house itself? Very little.' He gave a shrug of those broad shoulders. 'For the land it stands upon? Extensive.'

Gemini continued to stare at him, her expression remaining blank even as her thoughts inwardly raced. Bartholomew House was a beautiful three-hundred-year-old four-storey mansion house, standing on half an acre of prime land in the very heart of fashionable London. Land that Drakon Lyonedes seemed to be implying was his main reason for the purchase.

If that was so, then what did he intend doing with the house that stood on that piece of land?

'Oh, my God!' Gemini gasped weakly even as she felt the colour draining from her cheeks. 'You intend to have the house knocked down!'

Drakon scowled darkly as he heard the shocked accusation in her tone.

It was not an entirely incorrect accusation...

CHAPTER FOUR

'PERHAPS you should sit down before you fall down!' Drakon rasped harshly as he clasped the white-faced Gemini's arm to steady her before gently guiding her across the room to sit down in one of the armchairs. Putting his hand at the back of her neck, he pushed her head down between her knees.

Just what he needed. An unconscious Gemini Bartholomew in his apartment!

'Breathe deeply,' he instructed gruffly. The hand he held against the slenderness of her nape revealed that she was shaking. Badly!

Breathe deeply? Gemini wasn't sure how she could be expected to breathe at all when he had just revealed that his company intended destroying the house that had been in her family for hundreds of years! The same house where she had been born and had spent such a happy and carefree childhood…

'Drink this.'

Gemini raised her head enough to see the full glass of white wine Drakon now held in front of her, reaching up to take it from him before downing the contents in one go. 'Could I have some more, please?' she breathed shakily.

'I do not think—'

'Drakon, please!' Gemini rallied enough to look up at him pleadingly through the curtain of her hair.

He shrugged those broad shoulders before taking the empty glass from her shaking fingers and once again crossing over to the bar to refill it. 'I merely wished to point out that your drinking too much wine will not change anything.' He walked slowly back across the room.

Gemini's hands shook as she pushed her hair back over her shoulders before taking the refilled glass from him. 'I don't think I particularly care about that at the moment.'

He raised dark brows. 'Which, unfortunately, will not prevent you from suffering a hangover tomorrow morning.'

She laid her head back against the chair, breathing deeply. 'At this moment I'm more than happy to let tomorrow take care of itself!' She frowned suddenly. 'Are you even able to *legally* demolish a house as old Bartholomew?'

That square jaw tightened. 'Not completely, no.'

'What does that mean?'

He seemed to choose his words carefully. 'It means that our plans for the redevelopment of the site have, by necessity, to incorporate the original house.'

Gemini's heart sank. 'Incorporate it how, precisely?'

He shrugged. 'Plans have already been submitted and approved for the building of a hotel and conference centre.'

Gemini's hand tightened about her wine glass as she felt a sudden wave of dizziness. 'And no doubt Angela has known about these plans from the beginning?'

Drakon drew in a deep breath before turning and walking away, his back towards her as he looked out of one of the floor-to-ceiling windows. 'I believe your stepmother was made fully aware of our intentions at the outset, yes…'

Gemini would just bet that she was! She was sure Angela had been aware of it and no doubt inwardly gloated about it! It wasn't enough that she now owned the home that she knew full well Gemini had wanted for herself; the other woman was selling Bartholomew House to Lyonedes Enterprises knowing it was that company's intention to totally change, if not obliterate, the house and grounds as Gemini knew them…

'Intentions that I assure you I would have done everything in my power to block if I had known of them!' she cried.

'No doubt.'

'It would appear that I'm only just in time to present you with my own offer.'

Drakon's eyes narrowed as he turned slowly, allowing none of the regret he felt at seeing Gemini so pale and obviously distressed to show in the deliberate blandness of his expression. Which didn't mean that at that moment he wouldn't have liked to strangle Angela Bartholomew with his bare hands for being the initial cause of that distress!

He'd had no idea of the rift that existed between the two Bartholomew women when he'd entered into negotiations for the family house and grounds. Not that it would ultimately have made the slightest difference to those negotiations—but he usually made a point of being aware of any extraneous circumstances in his company's dealings.

He did not particularly care for the way Gemini now looked at him as if he were about to commit murder! 'What sort of offer?' he asked.

She stood up, only to sway slightly on her feet as the effects of the wine she had just consumed kicked in. 'Do you have a bread roll or something that I could eat?' she asked self-consciously.

Drakon gave an impatient sigh. 'We will sit down and eat dinner. Afterwards you will tell me about this offer you wish to make me.'

Sit down and eat dinner? Gemini felt as if even attempting to eat the bread roll she had requested would probably choke her! 'I think we've gone well past the stage of politely eating dinner together, don't you, Drakon?' she said dully.

'Then I suggest we *impolitely* eat dinner together.' He pulled one of the chairs back from the table and looked at her pointedly.

She gave a humourless smile as she walked slowly across the room and sat down abruptly in that chair. 'It might be as well if you gave lighting the candles a miss,' she advised heavily.

He nodded as he stepped round the table and began to take food from the hostess trolley and place it in front of her. 'We will not talk again until you have eaten something,' he assured her gruffly as he sat down opposite her.

For all the notice Gemini took of the meal—smoked salmon, followed by individual beef Wellingtons and tiny roasted vegetables, with some intricate chocolate confection to finish—Drakon might as well not have bothered putting it in front of her. Gemini was only able to chew disconsolately on a bread roll as she remained lost in the misery of imagining the beauty of Bartholomew House swallowed up by a hotel complex. It was unthinkable—unacceptable that such a thing should be allowed to happen.

True to his word, Drakon remained silent throughout, only speaking again once they had reached the coffee stage of their meal.

'It's decaffeinated,' he assured her as he placed a cup on the table in front of her.

At any other time, under different circumstances, Gemini would have felt warmed that a man like Drakon Lyonedes had bothered to remember her preference in coffee. Under *very* different circumstances! 'Thank you,' she accepted woodenly, before taking a sip of the black unsweetened brew.

'You're welcome,' he muttered as he resumed his seat opposite her.

'I can't exactly claim to have enjoyed my meal,' she said apologetically.

He shrugged. 'Luckily the chef of my favourite London restaurant is not here to be offended by the fact that you did not eat any of the food he so expertly provided.'

Gemini shot him a frowning glance. 'I could kick myself now for not realising Angela was up to something underhand after she refused my own offer to buy Bartholomew House from her.'

Drakon's brows rose. 'You made her an official offer for Bartholomew House?'

'Oh, yes,' she said. 'Angela just laughed in my face.'

The more Drakon heard about Angela Bartholomew the more he disliked her. And he would certainly have preferred to be more prepared for the distress caused to Gemini by her stepmother's mercenary nature.

He chose his words carefully. 'Admirable as your actions were, I doubt the amount you offered even came close to the offer Lyonedes Enterprises made to your stepmother—'

'I made sure the amount I offered slightly topped yours,' Gemini assured him firmly.

Drakon's eyes widened. 'You have *that* sort of money at your disposal?'

'More or less.'

His mouth twisted ruefully at the way that sea-green gaze now avoided meeting his. 'How much more and how much less?'

Gemini stood up restlessly. 'I *do* have the money,' she reiterated distractedly.

Drakon's lids narrowed as he looked across at her searchingly, noting the glitter in those sea-green eyes, the flush to her cheeks. And the determined set to that full and sensuous mouth...

Under different circumstances he could imagine nothing he would have enjoyed more than making love to Gemini until those sea-green eyes became heavy with desire, her cheeks flushed with pleasure, and those pouting lips swollen with arousal.

Under different circumstances...

As it was, even a hint of the sexual interest he felt for her, which had been growing steadily throughout the evening and intensifying to a physical ache when he'd placed his hand against her nape earlier, would be completely rejected.

Drakon couldn't remember the last time—if ever—a woman had piqued his sexual interest as much as Gemini did. If he were completely honest with himself she had begun to do so from the first moment he'd looked at her on the security monitor this morning, as she'd restlessly paced the room she had been confined to. Markos—damn him—had been quite correct in surmising as much when Drakon had announced it was his intention to talk to Gemini himself. His cousin had also known exactly which buttons to push to get a reaction out of Drakon when he had come up to the apartment and interrupted their conversation.

Drakon had been as surprised as Markos had looked when he had announced that Gemini was to be having dinner with him this evening. Surprised by the need he had felt to reassure her that he was not, nor had he ever been, involved in an affair with her stepmother. And not a little alarmed that the circumstances of their meeting meant he was the very last man Gemini would ever consider becoming sexually involved with.

Over the years Drakon had become accustomed to having any woman he bothered to take an interest in. The cynical part of him knew those conquests were due as much to his extreme wealth as to any personal attraction he may or may not possess, but he already knew Gemini well enough to know that neither his wealth nor the way he looked would be enough to tempt her into a purely physical relationship with him. She was a woman who would require...*more*...

Which left him precisely where?

Attracted—deeply attracted—to a woman he knew there was absolutely no possibility would ever return that attraction, let alone act upon it!

'You do have the money, *but*?' he prompted shrewdly.

Gemini shot him a frown. 'What makes you think there's a but?'

He gave a derisive smile. 'Isn't there?'

Yes, there was. And it was a big one. One that Gemini had desperately been trying to overcome this past month without success...

She sighed. 'I told you earlier that my parents set up a considerable trust fund for me. The interest has been paid to me on a yearly basis since I reached the age of eighteen, and the capital amount is to be made over to me on my thirtieth birthday.' She grimaced. 'I've been trying for the past month to see if I can break that trust and have the capital now, so that I can buy Bartholomew House.'

'And?'

She scowled. 'My father's lawyers assure me the trust was set up in such a way as to be unbreakable. Of course if Daddy had made the new will, as he promised he would…!' She gave a frustrated shake of her head. 'But obviously he didn't, so I'm stuck with not being able to get at the bulk of my money until my thirtieth birthday.'

Dark brows rose over those coal black eyes. 'Which means you will not receive the capital for…what…? Another three years or so?'

'Two years and four months, to be exact,' Gemini acknowledged grudgingly.

Drakon gave a humourless smile. 'By all means let us be exact—' He broke off, a perplexed frown appearing between his eyes. 'That would make your birthday some time in October?'

She nodded warily. 'The twenty-second.'

'But that is not the month for Gemini.'

Her wariness proved merited! 'No…'

'I had assumed your unusual name derived from your birth sign?'

Gemini forced a bright and totally insincere smile to her lips. 'Obviously you assumed wrong.'

Drakon studied her through narrowed eyes, noting that smile and the dull flatness of those sea-green eyes… 'You are being evasive, Gemini.'

'Am I?'

'You know that you are.'

Her expression was pained as she began to pace, slender and long-legged and extremely graceful, her hair a silvery curtain about her shoulders in the moonlight reflecting through the windows behind her.

'I don't see what my birthday has do with the offer I've made you—'

'You have not made me any offer yet—nor do I wish to hear it until we have finished our present conversation,' Drakon assured her decisively as she would have gone on. 'Gemini is the sign of the twins...' he murmured slowly.

The frown deepened between those sea-green eyes. 'Most people would have realised by now—and *accepted*—that I would obviously prefer not to talk about this subject any more!' she muttered crossly.

He nodded. 'I have realised.'

'But you continued anyway?'

'Yes.'

'Why?' she demanded.

Because, painful as he could see this subject was to her, Drakon wanted—*needed*—to know!

She had told him so much about herself already— when her birthday was, what she did for a living, her love for her parents, her disharmonious relationship with her stepmother. And it wasn't enough. Drakon found that he desired to know all that there was to know about Gemini Bartholomew. Almost as much as he desired to make love to her...

'I'm a twin,' she revealed suddenly, her eyes glittering brightly with unshed tears as she turned away. 'I had a brother,' she continued quietly. 'He only lived for three hours after he was born, and my mother chose my name deliberately—not out of the sadness of losing him, but out of the joy of knowing him even for that short amount of time. She didn't want any of us to ever forget him—' Gemini broke off abruptly as her voice choked with tears. The silken curtain of her hair fell forward to hide the depth of emotion so clearly revealed in the rawness of her voice.

Drakon gave a self-disgusted snort and moved swiftly across the room. He took Gemini into his arms, resting her head against his shoulder, and moved his arms firmly about the slenderness of her waist, her closeness allowing him to breathe in the soft perfume of her hair. 'I am so sorry, Gemini,' he muttered. 'You were right. I should not have pushed you in the way I did.'

'No, it's okay.' She shook her head. 'I— It's just that since Daddy died there's no one left who knew about Gabriel—that was my brother's name. Gabriel. Gemini and Gabriel.' She drew in a ragged breath. 'It's strange, because I never really knew him, but I've always felt as if…as if I were somehow incomplete…as if a part of me were missing.' She looked up to give a tearful smile. 'Weird, huh?'

Not weird at all when one considered that Gabriel had been her twin—that the two of them had shared their mother's womb for nine months at the very beginning of their lives…

It also explained that sadness Drakon had recognised earlier in the beauty of Gemini's eyes when he had mentioned there being no son to inherit her father's business. Because he now realised there had been no *living* son…

Gemini had no brother living. No parents, either. Leaving her completely alone in the world.

Much as Markos's flirtatious nature often annoyed him, and much as he sometimes grew concerned about his widowed mother spending months living alone in

Athens, Drakon knew he couldn't imagine being without either of them.

His hand seemed to move of its own volition to touch the softness of her hair. 'I think that is a perfectly natural feeling in the circumstances,' he said as he stroked that silkiness.

Those sea-green eyes widened as she breathed, 'You do?'

'Of course.' Drakon nodded, entwining several of those silky strands about his long fingers. 'I have considered Markos as my brother since I was ten years old, and we have always been close. To know that you could have had that same closeness with your own brother must be difficult sometimes. Especially this past six months, with both your parents now gone too.'

Gemini had no idea what she was doing, virtually spilling out her life history to Drakon Lyonedes of all people! Having only met him for the first time this morning, and having found him so remote and arrogantly sure of himself, she would have thought him the last person she would be confiding her inner emotions to only hours later!

Even more worrying was the fact that she was now completely physically aware of him…

Not that she hadn't been aware of his dark and dangerous good looks from the moment she first looked at him—what woman wouldn't be? But being this close to him…held tightly in his arms, with her body moulded against the lean and muscled hardness of his…every part of her, all her senses, seemed to be screaming with that awareness.

He smelled so good—clean and virile male, with a spicy and insidiously delicious cologne. And his body felt so warm and solid against her own. Those shoulders wide and muscled, his chest and stomach powerfully lean, his long legs placed solidly either side of hers, his thighs hard and—

Oh, help…!

Gemini tensed even as she looked up at Drakon through lowered lashes, barely breathing as she felt the press of his arousal against the softness of her stomach. She was only a few inches shorter than him in her heels, and their faces were even closer as the warmth of his breath brushed against her cheek. There was no doubting that Drakon was aware of that sudden sexual tension too. His jaw was clenched, a nerve pulsing in that tightness, his mouth was compressed and his cheekbones high and prominent. And those dark eyes—

Those dark eyes were burning with the same desire Gemini could feel pressing so insistently against her!

What did she do now? To act on the aching desire flooding her limbs and so desperately clamouring for her to close the distance that separated their parted lips would be asking for trouble. To pull away and run wasn't really an option either, when they still had so much to talk about.

Drakon suddenly solved her dilemma by grasping the tops of her arms and putting her firmly away from him before stepping back.

'Better now?' he prompted coolly. The emotion in those coal-black eyes was now shielded behind hooded lids, his expression once again arrogantly remote as he lifted his glass and took a swallow of the white wine.

Well, Gemini could breathe again, at least! It remained to be seen whether or not she would be able to put that physical awareness behind her as thoroughly as he appeared to have done. 'Much,' she confirmed huskily. 'Thank you.'

Drakon had no idea what Gemini was thanking him for. Allowing her to talk of her family, perhaps? Or the fact that he had decided not to act on the sexual tension that minutes ago had thickened the air in the room to an almost unbearable degree?

It was a sexual tension he would normally not have hesitated to act upon, but in Gemini's case, here and now, it could only have seemed like taking advantage of her vulnerability…

Drakon knew himself to be many things—controlled, arrogant, ruthless—but until this moment he would not have thought self-denial to be a part of his nature. It was a self-denial he would no doubt live to regret if the throbbing ache of his erection was any indication!

He arched arrogant dark brows as he turned. 'For what?'

Gemini shrugged. 'Being a shoulder to lean on when I needed one.'

'I did nothing except listen,' he dismissed abruptly as he placed the empty wine glass back down on the table. 'And I believe it is now time for me to listen to you, as you make your offer to me with regard to Bartholomew House. The same as that you made to your stepmother?' he reminded her.

Gemini looked at him searchingly for several long seconds, but could see nothing of the compassionate and caring man of seconds ago in the harsh implacability of Drakon's expression. The obviously aroused man who had held her in his arms only seconds ago had also gone.

She gave a rueful shake of her head. 'My offer is to Lyonedes Enterprises rather than to Drakon Lyonedes…'

His mouth tightened. 'It is one and the same thing.'

'Not really,' Gemini pointed out. 'Lyonedes Enterprises doesn't consist of just you, does it? There's your cousin to consider, too.'

He looked down the length of his arrogant nose at her. 'My cousin, I assure you, will be more than willing to accept my judgement, as I accept his, in all matters relating to Lyonedes Enterprises.'

Gemini would just bet he would! She had no doubt that not too many people ever went up against this man in any of his decisions—not even the cousin he was obviously so close to. Not in the way that *she* had done today.

Now that she had actually met and spoken with Drakon she realised she was lucky his Head of Security hadn't decided to lock her in the basement this morning after all—and thrown away the key!

'Okay.' She drew in a deep breath. 'My offer to Angela in buying Bartholomew House was that I'd pay over the interest from my trust fund for the next two years, and the remaining amount once the capital was released on my thirtieth birthday. I'm willing to make Lyonedes Enterprises the same offer once the property becomes yours.'

It was exactly the offer that Drakon had been expecting Gemini to make, after hearing the details of her trust fund.

And an offer he had no choice but to refuse on behalf of Lyonedes Enterprises.

CHAPTER FIVE

GEMINI knew what Drakon's answer to her offer was going to be even before he spoke—could see that answer as she looked into those remorseless black eyes.

'Yes. Well. Obviously not.' She moved quickly to pick up her clutch bag from the arm of the chair where she had left it earlier, her face pale in the lamplight. 'I think it's past time I was going, anyway. I'm sorry to have wasted your time.' She turned away.

'Gemini!'

She froze before turning slowly back to face Drakon. 'Yes?'

Drakon scowled at the brief flash of hope he saw in those in those sea-green eyes. 'I cannot let you leave when you are so obviously upset.'

'I don't see how you're planning on stopping me.' She looked at him quizzically. 'Look, Drakon.' She sighed wearily as he continued to scowl his displeasure. 'It's obvious that you aren't any more interested in the deal I'm offering than Angela was, so I think it's best if I just be on my way now. It will save us both the embarrassment of your having to say so.'

No. Unfortunately Drakon could not in all conscience even *consider* a deal in which Lyonedes Enterprises effectively paid out millions of pounds for a prime site the company wanted in the heart of London, then shelved their idea to build a hotel complex there in favour of selling it on to Gemini, who would then pay them back in instalments. From a business point of view the whole idea was ludicrous!

And from a personal one…?

Drakon frowned darkly as he saw the look of defeat in the pallor of Gemini's face. Her eyes now appeared like huge sea-green lakes of bleak despair against that paleness. Because she now knew beyond a shadow of a doubt that she had lost the family home she so obviously loved. The last tie with the father she had also loved and so recently lost…

He gave an impatient shake of his head, knowing that he couldn't back down on his decision. Not only was it the right one in regard to Lyonedes Enterprises, it would be totally against his nature to do so. 'I do not believe for one moment that your father intended your trust fund to be used for such a purpose.'

She gave him a bitter smile. 'We'll never know now what he intended, will we?'

Drakon's jaw tightened. 'The fact that he did not, as he intended, make a new will, perhaps implies that he had rethought his decision to leave you Bartholomew House?'

'Oh, please, Drakon!' Gemini threw him a fiery glance. 'As you didn't even know my father you can have absolutely no idea what he did or didn't decide.'

He winced at the emotion in her voice. 'That is not completely true. I met your father several times at social functions in London over the years.'

That was news to Gemini. Although there was absolutely no reason why her father should ever have mentioned meeting the legendary Drakon Lyonedes to her.

He couldn't have known that Gemini and Drakon would meet one day. Especially under these circumstances!

'And?'

He shrugged those wide shoulders. 'And he always seemed a man of decisiveness and purpose.'

Gemini smiled sadly. 'Then I can only assume you must have met him pre-Angela.'

'Perhaps,' Drakon acknowledged. 'But from a practical point of view what would you even *do* with a home and grounds the size of Bartholomew House? Surely it is far too big for you to have considered living there alone?'

Her stubbornly pointed chin rose. 'I have—*had*,' she corrected firmly, 'no intention of living there alone, Drakon.'

Ah. It was a complication Drakon hadn't but definitely should have considered before now… 'You are engaged. Or intend to be married soon?'

'Of course not.' She looked down pointedly at her bare left hand before adding, 'I wouldn't be here having dinner alone with you if I was!' She shook her head. 'But I don't intend always to be alone. I would like to be married at some time in the future, and to have children of my own one day. Whenever I've envisaged that day I've always thought I would be living in Bartholomew House,' she said huskily.

Guilt was not an emotion Drakon was in the least familiar with, and it now sat uncomfortably heavy on his shoulders. Especially when it was in connection with a young woman he found altogether too attractive for his own comfort! Nor was he particularly happy with the brief feeling of satisfaction he had experienced at knowing Gemini was not seriously involved with anyone else at the moment. The chances of her ever becoming involved with *him*, now that he had refused even to consider her proposal for purchasing Bartholomew House, were also extremely remote!

He looked across at her through narrowed lids. 'I don't see how anyone could have reason to object to your having a business dinner with me?'

Gemini accepted that it might have started out as a business dinner—except for the subdued lighting and those candles on the dinner table—but Drakon certainly hadn't been feeling businesslike a few minutes ago, when she had felt the evidence of his arousal pressing against her. When whether or not they kissed each other had hung so delicately in the balance for several tense and breathlessly expectant moments!

'Probably not,' she accepted briskly. 'But I wouldn't have felt right about coming here if I was involved with someone.'

Drakon frowned his irritation. 'I don't see why not. Or is it your intention, when this "one day" arrives with this as yet imaginary husband and children, to close yourself off from all other social contact?'

'Of course not.' Gemini gave him a derisive glance. 'But going out for the evening to have dinner alone with—well, frankly with another man, who happens to be single and very eligible, really isn't acceptable when you're married to someone else.'

He raised dark brows. 'Even if it is a business dinner?'

'Even then.' She shrugged dismissively. 'I wouldn't be at all happy knowing my husband was out to dinner with some glamorous blonde or brunette, business or otherwise, so I wouldn't expect him to like my doing it either. And I really have no idea why we are even talking about someone who doesn't even exist yet,' she added wryly. 'It's bizarre!'

It was an odd conversation, Drakon acknowledged. One that gave him even more of an insight into the type of woman Gemini Bartholomew was.

At the same time it reiterated his earlier impression that she was not the type of woman to enter lightly into what Drakon already knew, from that brief time of holding her in his arms, would be a highly volatile sexual affair between the two of them. Indeed, she was the type of woman who would need to be in love, rather than just in lust, with any man she went to bed with.

Surely that didn't mean she might still be a virgin at twenty-seven?

Of course it didn't; just because Gemini hadn't married yet it didn't mean she hadn't already fallen in—and out—of love, or had sex. Or *made love*, as she no doubt thought of it!

Drakon's hands clenched at his sides just at the thought of other men making love to her. Of those men having seen her naked, with that beautiful white-gold hair falling caressingly over them as they touched and kissed all those delectable and willowy curves—

Those regrets at his earlier self-denial had occurred even more quickly than Drakon had imagined they might!

He nodded abruptly. 'I will ring for the car and have you driven back to your home,' he said.

'There's no need,' Gemini replied. 'I can easily get a taxi once I'm outside.'

'I arranged for your transport here, and as such cannot possibly allow you to go home in a taxi,' he bit out harshly.

'You aren't *allowing* me to do anything, Drakon.'

Gemini couldn't help smiling a little at his arrogance. 'And I want to go now,' she insisted heavily, that humour quickly fading. 'Not in ten minutes or so when the car arrives.'

He straightened. 'Then I will drive you home myself—'

'That really isn't necessary.' She frowned at the mere idea of being confined in a car with him for the fifteen minutes or so it would take to drive her back to her apartment. Drakon had rejected her offer, and now she just wanted to get out of here—not drag this awkwardness out a moment longer. 'Nor is it a good idea, considering you've been drinking wine—the licensing laws over here are pretty strict.' She drew in a deep breath. 'Thank you for dinner—'

'Which you were too upset to eat.' A nerve pulsed in the tightness of his jaw.

'And the lovely wine—which I certainly wasn't too upset to drink,' she added pointedly. 'And for listening to me, at least…'

Drakon scowled his displeasure at the frown that had reappeared between those magnificent eyes. 'There really is no reason for you to leave so soon—'

'I'm afraid there's every reason, Drakon.' Gemini sighed. 'You were my last hope, I'm afraid.'

He knew that, and inwardly railed against the fact that he had ultimately proved to be so unhelpful to her. But, apart from his immediate family, business had always come first and last with him—certainly for the ten years since he had taken over as President of Lyonedes Enterprises. The appeal of a beautiful pair of sea-green eyes and the allure of a desirable body simply were not justifiable reasons for him to give even a moment's consideration to Gemini's impractical offer to purchase Bartholomew House.

'I will need to come down in the lift with you, at least, in order to let you out of the building,' he rasped.

'By all means come downstairs and see me off the premises,' she accepted teasingly. 'Having already been confined by your security man once today, I would hate for it to happen a second time—and maybe this time involve the police because all the alarms go off as I try to leave!'

As the two of them stepped into the lift together Drakon couldn't help but admire Gemini's cool dignity only minutes after he had dealt her what must have been a devastating blow. Many women, as he knew from experience, would have resorted to shrieking or crying—or even seduction—in order to try and get their own way, but not Gemini Bartholomew. There was no doubting she looked slightly more emotionally fragile than when she had arrived, but otherwise her calm dignity was still firmly in place.

Not that any of those things would have worked where Drakon was concerned—although the seduction would no doubt have been enjoyable. But Gemini had not even tried to exert *any* of her feminine wiles on him.

Was that disappointment Drakon felt? Possibly. In the circumstances, he could not in all conscience act upon his own desires, but having Gemini act upon her sexual awareness of *him*, which he had sensed in her such a short time ago, would have been a different matter entirely!

Gemini was very aware of Drakon standing beside her as they went down in the lift together. And of a return of that sexual tension that had occurred earlier when he had taken her in his arms. If it had ever gone away…

If she were honest with herself, she hadn't really held out much hope of Drakon being receptive to her unusual offer to buy Bartholomew House from Lyonedes Enterprises when she'd agreed to have dinner with him this evening. She had already realised that from a business point of view it really wasn't a very practical offer. So having Drakon turn down the offer had come as no real surprise.

The physical awareness that had sprung so readily to life between them earlier and was still so tangibly evident most definitely had…

Oh, Gemini wasn't surprised that she found Drakon physically attractive—she had realised when she met him this morning that he was a dangerously handsome man!—but that Drakon so obviously found *her* physically attractive too had come as a total shock. She wouldn't have thought she was his type at all—too determined and pushy, too impulsive, and definitely far too outspoken.

If she had thought about it at all she would have imagined that the sort of woman he found attractive would be someone undemanding and elegantly beautiful, with a social charm that acted as a foil for his own more taciturn nature. Someone that her stepmother Angela was only too capable of at least pretending to be. As Gemini knew only too well, Angela's true nature was only revealed after a wedding!

Gemini looked at Drakon from beneath lowered lashes, aware that her breathing had become shallow and her body hot. Her breasts felt full and heavy, the nipples hard and sensitive pebbles, and a telling dampness was flooding her thighs as she wondered what it

would be like to make love with such a vitally powerful and ruggedly handsome man. She had absolutely no
doubt that Drakon would be a deeply satisfying and accomplished lover—that he would be as accomplished at
lovemaking as she had so naively commented he probably was on the piano!

Come to think of it, there were quite a few similari-
ties between making love and playing the piano—surely
it was all a question of running your fingers over the
right keys in order to achieve the most satisfying result?
In fact—

'What are you doing?' Gemini gasped as the lights
flickered and the lift came to a sudden halt between
floors. Drakon had reached out and pressed one of the
buttons on the panel before turning to look at her, his
expression as dark and unreadable as his eyes as he
looked down at her for several tension-filled seconds.
'Drakon…?' She looked up at him dazedly.

Drakon reached out and took Gemini in his arms.
He moulded the softness of her body against his hardness, aware that she wanted this as much as he did as
he heard the shallowness of her breathing, saw the swell
of her breasts above her dress, the nipples hard against
the softness of that material, and felt the warmth of the
rest of her body instinctively curve intimately into his.

'Drakon…?' She sounded slightly panicked now, as
he studied her intently before moving one of his hands
to cup the side of her face, to gently part the softness
of her lips. The soft pad of his thumb dipped into the
heated moisture of her mouth before slowly spreading
that moisture across her lips. 'Drakon…!' she gasped
weakly, and she allowed her bag to slide to the floor of
the lift and her arms to move about his waist beneath
his jacket.

Her hands were warm against his back through the silk of his shirt. It was all the encouragement he needed to lower his head and capture the moistness of her lips with his, groaning low in his throat as those lips parted further and the kiss deepened. Their ragged breathing sounded loud in the still silence of the dimly lit lift as the two of them sucked and bit on each other's lips as they kissed hungrily, passionately.

Drakon only lifted his lips from hers in order to taste the creaminess of her throat as he pushed her back against the wall of the lift and ground the hard and aching throb of his arousal against her. She tasted of warmth and honey, of arousal, and her skin was hot against his lips as he kissed his way down to the swell of her breasts, tasting and licking her there, muttering his dissatisfaction as the fitted bodice of her dress prevented him from going lower.

Gemini was so aroused, so lost in the pleasure of Drakon's kisses and caresses, that she wasn't even aware of his having lowered the zip at the back of her dress and tugged aside the material until she felt his lips against the bareness of her breasts. His tongue was a moist rasp across her nipple before he drew that sensitive peak deep into the heat of his mouth. Her hands grasped his shoulders for support as his fingers cupped her other breast and his thumb moved across it in the same rhythmic caress, causing a warm rush of moisture to pool and dampen between her thighs.

Drakon continued to grind the hardness of his arousal against her and her breath caught in her throat, her arousal tightening to fever pitch as she looked down at him, his lashes long and dark against the olive skin of his hollowed cheeks, those firm and ruthless lips parted over her nipple as he drew on her deeply, hungrily, his teeth biting into the softness of her flesh, his tongue a rough and erotic scrape of pleasure.

She gave a whimper of protest as his lips and tongue reluctantly released that turgid nipple, only to moan low in her throat as he turned their attention to her other breast. Her fingers became entangled in the darkness of his hair as the ache between her thighs intensified to a burn of need that caused her to shift restlessly against the long length of his shaft, crying out softly as she felt his hardness rub against her swollen flesh through the fine fabric of their clothes, groaning, gasping, as she continued to move rhythmically against him, feeling herself spiralling out of control as the intensity, the depth of pleasure, hurtled her towards release.

'Hello? Mr Lyonedes? Do you need assistance?'

Gemini stiffened dazedly and Drakon stilled against her breast as that intrusive voice pierced the heat of their arousal.

'Mr Lyonedes? Do you require assistance, sir?'

Gemini recognised the voice as belonging to Max, the Head of Security for Lyonedes Enterprises she had met that morning, even as Drakon released her abruptly before stepping away from her.

His expression was tight and extremely grim as he looked down at her darkly for several seconds, before turning away to lift the receiver beside the lit panel. 'No assistance needed, Max,' he barked into the mouthpiece.

'Are you sure, sir? The lift appears to be stuck between the thirteenth and fourteenth floors…?'

'Not stuck, Max, just not moving,' he assured the other man tautly. 'Miss Bartholomew and I will be descending to the ground floor in a few moments.'

There was a brief, telling silence before the other man spoke again. 'Very good. Thank you, sir.'

'Miss Bartholomew' had quickly pulled up the bodice of her dress while Drakon spoke to his Head of Security, the heat now in her cheeks due to intense embarrassment rather than arousal. Not only had she almost made love with Drakon in a lift—which was surely mortifying enough?—but after that brief conversation with his employer, no doubt Max was also fully aware of exactly why the lift had been stopped between floors!

Good Lord, she had almost made love with *Drakon* in a *lift*!

Drakon Lyonedes...

Even more frustratingly, his hair smoothed back into style and his suit jacket and tie now straightened, he now looked just as smoothly self-contained as usual. Whereas she—goodness knew what she must look like, with her dress still unzipped at the back and her hair in a tangle about her shoulders, her cheeks hot and the peach gloss kissed from her lips!

'Turn around.'

Gemini raised startled lids and looked warily up at Drakon. She moistened her slightly swollen and sensitive lips before speaking. 'Sorry...?'

His own mouth was a thin, uncompromising line in the arrogant planes of his face, his eyes as hard as the onyx they resembled. 'If you turn around I will re-zip your dress.'

Gemini clutched the material to her breasts and quickly turned away from him, trembling when she felt every cold inch of that zip against her heated skin as Drakon deftly refastened it. She wondered what on earth she was supposed to do now... How was she supposed to behave towards the man she had almost made love with in a lift? Was there a precedent for that sort of thing? Some sort of protocol that she—never having made love in a lift before—didn't have a clue about?

Of course there wasn't a protocol for this type of thing! And hysteria really wasn't an option either—which meant Gemini had to get a grip as quickly as possible and stop behaving like an inexperienced idiot. Even if she was one…

Oh, she had dated often at university—had even thought she might have been in love a couple of times and mildly experimented with lovemaking. But once she'd bought and started to run the shop her time had pretty much been taken up with making it into a success, leaving little opportunity for dating, let alone falling in love. In fact, now that she gave it some thought, dinner this evening with Drakon was as close as she had got to having anything that even resembled a date for well over a year.

Which was absolutely no excuse—and definitely not an explanation—for the explosion of arousal and passion that had just happened between the two of them!

She might be inexperienced, but Drakon certainly wasn't. And after her behaviour just now she doubted that he would believe she was either…

'Do you intend to stare at that wall for the rest of our journey down?'

Gemini flinched at the hard amusement she could hear in Drakon's voice as she felt the lift begin its descent. 'Not at all,' she denied briskly, and she turned, bending down to retrieve her clutch bag from the floor of the lift before forcing herself to look up and meet the hardness of his gaze. 'Well, that was certainly…different,' she said lamely.

'Yes.' Drakon's mouth twisted in self-derision. 'Different' was certainly one way of describing the way in which the situation had totally spiralled out of his control once he had taken Gemini into his arms!

He hadn't meant to kiss her at all, let alone touch her in that intimate way, but once he had done so and she had responded…! It hadn't mattered to Drakon at all that at that moment they were in a lift together. Nor had he given any thought to the fact that stopping the lift in between floors in that way would alert whoever was on security duty this evening. He had just wanted to touch her, taste her—damn it, he had wanted to eat her up until he had totally devoured her! He still wanted to do that…

His jaw tightened. 'I do not fly back to New York until next week. Perhaps we could have dinner together again tomorrow evening?'

Those beautiful sea-green eyes widened incredulously. 'I don't think that's a good idea, do you?'

Drakon raised dark brows. 'Why not?'

Gemini shook her head. 'I'm sure I don't really have to explain that to you!' She glanced gratefully out into the hallway as the lift doors opened out onto the ground floor.

'Nevertheless…' Drakon stood back to allow her to precede him out into the dimmed hallway, his expression grim. 'We have already established that neither of us is involved with anyone else.'

That might or might not be true—the fact that Gemini had believed Drakon when he'd claimed not to be involved with Angela didn't mean that he didn't have someone else waiting for him in New York! And it certainly didn't mean that they should see each other again before he left England.

Not when agreeing to see him again would no doubt be seen by him as a tacit agreement from her for a repeat—no, a *conclusion* of that explosion of passion that had just occurred between them in the lift…

CHAPTER SIX

GEMINI gave a definite shake of her head. 'I'm sure to be exhausted after working on the wedding flowers all day tomorrow, but thank you for asking.'

Drakon had regretted making the invitation virtually as soon as he'd made it! Regretted it and inwardly berated himself for even *thinking* of seeing her again.

This woman had a way of slipping beneath his guard. Of totally demolishing the tight rein he always kept over his self-control. Of tempting him to behave in ways he never had before. If Max hadn't interrupted them when he had then Drakon had no doubt he would actually have made love to Gemini—in a lift, of all places!

It was unacceptable to a man who totally rejected any and all hint of emotional vulnerability, and instead preferred to remain detached and in control at all times. Wanting to push a woman up against a wall and make unbridled love to her couldn't be called either of those things!

No, it was better by far if Drakon never saw or spoke to her again. And after this evening there was absolutely no reason why he should ever need to do so...

'Very well.' He nodded stiffly. 'But I will come outside with you and see you safely into a taxi.'

Gemini could have argued that she had lived in

London all her life and as such was perfectly capable of seeing herself into a taxi, thank you very much! But no doubt Drakon would then argue the point, and delay her departure by doing so. Which she certainly didn't want when she so desperately needed to get away from him.

It wasn't in the least apparent from Drakon's cool and controlled expression as he looked down the length of his arrogant nose at her that only minutes ago he had almost made love to her with a fire and intimacy no other man ever had. But she was only too well aware of it. Her breasts still ached with sensitivity, and she could feel that telltale dampness between her thighs…

As was to be expected, there was no scarcity of available taxis when Drakon Lyonedes needed one, and he had no trouble flagging down one of London's black cabs almost immediately they stepped to the edge of the pavement; he was the type of man for whom life always ran the way in which he wanted it to.

Unlike Gemini, who had no choice but to accept that Bartholomew House was now totally beyond her reach.

She felt numbed and slightly hollow as she climbed into the back of the taxi, only half listening as Drakon leant in to give the driver the address of her apartment.

'I can be contacted through my cousin Markos if you ever have need of me.'

Gemini blinked up at Drakon from the back seat of the taxi. Why would he suppose she might ever have need of him? 'Managing to speak to one of the Lyonedes family didn't work out too well for me last time,' she reminded him pointedly, just wanting to be on her way so that she could lick her wounds in private.

All her wounds. Losing Bartholomew House *and* responding so uninhibitedly to this grim-faced man's earlier passion. At the moment she wasn't sure which of those things was going to be the more difficult to understand, let alone accept.

Drakon's mouth was set firmly. 'I will leave instructions that you are to be allowed to make an appointment to see either Markos or myself at any time.'

Gemini's eyes widened. 'Why on earth would you want to do that?'

A good question. And one that he wasn't sure he had a logical answer to. Except to say that his Greek upbringing did not find it acceptable that Gemini had effectively been left completely alone in the world since her father died.

'The instruction will be given,' he reiterated firmly. 'You may please yourself as to whether or not you ever choose to use the privilege.'

She sat back against the seat. 'I'm pretty sure that I won't.'

He had asked for that response, Drakon acknowledged ruefully, knowing that his present attitude was less than gracious. But this young woman had become like a burr under his skin—a discomfort he couldn't seem to ignore.

'I hope you do not have to work too hard tomorrow.' He stepped back and closed the door, leaving a pale-faced Gemini bathed only in moonlight as the taxi drew away from the kerb.

Drakon stood on the pavement and watched the taxi until its tail lights disappeared amongst the other London evening traffic, then turned sharply on his heel and went back into Lyonedes Tower, knowing—well, hoping—he had seen the last of Gemini Bartholomew...

* * *

'We may have a problem.'

Drakon looked up from where he had been packing the last of his papers into his briefcase in preparation for his flight back to New York early this evening, frowning as he saw the unhappy expression on Markos's face as his cousin came into the study of the penthouse apartment at the top of Lyonedes Tower.

'What sort of a problem?' Having spent a quiet weekend in the apartment in preparation for two days of lengthy negotiation with Thompson Oil—which had, of course, been concluded to Lyonedes Enterprises' advantage—Drakon wasn't in the mood to deal with any hiccups that might now have occurred in the finalising of that contract. Nothing which could threaten his return to New York today. He had been away from his own office for long enough.

Markos grimaced. 'Mrs Bartholomew came to see me this afternoon—'

'*Miss* Bartholomew,' Drakon corrected, wondering why, when he hadn't yet left the country, Gemini had chosen to make an appointment with Markos rather than himself. And for what reason… 'Gemini is not married.'

'If I'd meant Gemini then I would have said Gemini,' Markos reasoned impatiently.

Drakon eyed his cousin guardedly as he slowly stepped away from the desk. 'So it was her stepmother who came to see you today?'

His cousin nodded. 'Well, I had the distinct impression she would have preferred it to have been you, but as you weren't available this afternoon she settled for seeing me instead.'

Drakon had spent the past four days trying not to think about Gemini. Not too successfully, admittedly.

Several times he had found himself lost in thoughts of making love with her, and usually at the most inappropriate of times. The last thing he had been expecting was a visit to Lyonedes Tower by her stepmother.

'What did she want?'

'You. Or, alternatively, me.' Markos gave a disgusted snort.

He shook his head. 'Is there some problem with our purchase of the Bartholomew property?' Such as a more recent Miles Bartholomew will making a sudden and unexpected appearance? That would certainly solve all Gemini's problems—whilst at the same time opening up a legal nightmare for Lyonedes Enterprises!

'Not that I'm aware.' Markos immediately dismissed that possibility. 'Angela Bartholomew's interest in the Lyonedes family appeared to be completely personal,' he added, with a contemptuous curl of his top lip. 'She invited me out to dinner this evening,' he expanded when Drakon still looked nonplussed. 'And she left me in no doubt that dinner would very swiftly be followed by bed.'

It was so much in keeping with the things Gemini had implied if not said about her stepmother that Drakon found it difficult to hold his smile in check. 'And did you accept the invitation?'

'Don't be so damned stupid! Have you ever *met* the woman?' His cousin glared at Drakon's obvious amusement. 'She's a barracuda wrapped in designer-label silk!'

Drakon bit his top lip to stop his smile from deepening. 'I have had the...pleasure of meeting her once, yes. When the contracts were signed.'

'And?'

'She's a barracuda wrapped in designer-label silk,' he agreed.

'This isn't funny, Drakon.' Markos scowled. 'I thought it was a business meeting, and I was so surprised by the obvious sexual intent in her invitation that I'm afraid I was less than my usual discreet self.'

Drakon's humour instantly faded. 'What did you do?'

His cousin looked annoyed. 'I merely commented what a charming stepdaughter she has—at which she asked very sweetly when and how I had met her stepdaughter.'

'Did you tell her?' Drakon rasped sharply.

'At the time I didn't think there was any reason not to.'

'Exactly what did you tell her, Markos?' Drakon demanded.

'I said we had both met her when she came here last week to talk to you. That was when that sweetness completely disappeared and I saw the true nature of the woman.' Markos winced at the memory. 'I've never seen such a change in anyone. She was muttering something about killing her as she left.'

'How long ago was that?'

'Only ten minutes or so—where are you going?' Markos asked in surprise as Drakon strode forcefully towards the door.

He turned in the doorway. 'To ensure she does not succeed in harming Gemini, of course.'

His cousin raised dark brows. 'What about your flight?'

Drakon shrugged dismissively. 'If necessary I'll reschedule the jet for tomorrow. Right now I believe I need to go and ensure Gemini's safety.'

Markos looked shocked. 'You really think Angela Bartholomew would physically harm her?'

Drakon gave a humourless smile. 'From what I have learnt, I don't believe that woman needs to lay a finger on Gemini in order to hurt her. Or to enjoy every moment of doing so,' he added grimly.

'Do you want me to come with you? Probably not.' Markos raised placatory hands as Drakon turned to glare at him.

'I think you've already done enough for one day, don't you?' he asked accusingly.

'I really had no idea how she felt about Gemini until she changed from sex-kitten into tigress just at the mention of her name!' his cousin defended.

No, in all fairness, Markos *hadn't* known of the depth of animosity that existed between Gemini and her stepmother. Drakon had chosen to tell his cousin only the rudimentary details of the reason for her visit to him the previous week. And he had only told Markos that much out of self-defence—to illustrate that it had been a business meeting and nothing more—after his cousin had teased him over the weekend about whether or not he would be seeing Gemini again before he returned to New York.

Much as it irked Drakon to admit it even to himself, these past four days he had wanted to see her again. He had wanted it very much. Those occasions when he had been unable to succeed in putting her from his mind had usually resulted in him having to take a cold shower. Yes, Drakon had *really* wanted to see Gemini again.

He had just never imagined it would be under circumstances such as these...

* * *

'Exactly what did you think you were doing?'

Gemini had taken advantage of a brief lull in the day's business and left her assistant in charge of the shop while she retired to her office, intending to go through the accounts and check on the rest of the month's bookings. The last thing she had been expecting late on a Tuesday afternoon—or at any time, in fact—was a visit from Angela!

She drew in a deep breath before glancing up at her father's widow, not in the least reassured by the angry glitter she could see in Angela's eyes and the bright spots of colour in her cheeks. The rest of her appearance was as elegantly beautiful as usual; her hair was perfectly styled, the blue silk knee-length suit a perfect match in colour for her eyes, the three-inch heels on the matching shoes making her legs appear both slender and shapely. An elegantly beautiful viper!

'What did I think I was doing in regard to what?' Gemini enquired calmly as she placed her pen carefully down on the desktop in front of her.

'Don't try and play the innocent with me!' Angela snapped as she stepped fully into the office and slammed the door behind her before striding over to stand in front of the desk and look down at Gemini contemptuously. 'You've always acted so primly self-righteous. I never would have guessed that you would attempt something so underhand!'

Gemini looked at her blankly. 'Flattered as I am to have so obviously succeeded in surprising you, I still have absolutely no idea what you're talking about.'

Angela's pale blue gaze swept over her scornfully. 'You know exactly what I'm talking about.'

Her patience with this woman had worn thin long ago, and now that her father was dead, and Angela was selling everything he had ever worked for and owned, Gemini saw absolutely no reason why she should even attempt to hide her dislike any longer.

She stood up impatiently. 'If you don't tell me what you're doing here in the next few minutes then I'm afraid you'll leave me with no choice but to demand that you leave.'

Those blue eyes flashed angrily. 'Perhaps the name Drakon Lyonedes might help to jog your memory?'

Gemini felt the colour drain from her cheeks. Drakon? Angela was here because she *knew* Gemini had been to Lyonedes Tower to talk to him concerning Bartholomew House? Did Angela also know she'd had dinner with him there on Friday evening? That they'd kissed? And, if so, *how* did she know? Surely Angela could only have learnt those things from Drakon himself?

Did that mean he had been lying to her, after all, when he'd denied any personal involvement with Angela?

Gemini eyed the other woman guardedly. 'What about him?'

Angela gave an inelegant snort. 'I told you not to try and play the little innocent with me.' She looked daggers at Gemini. 'And to think Miles always believed you were such a sweet little thing too.'

'Whatever problem you think you have with me, you will leave my father out of this,' Gemini said, her hands clenched so tightly at her sides that her nails were digging painfully into her palms.

'Will I?' the older woman challenged derisively as she perched one slender hip against the side of the desk. 'I wonder what Miles would have thought about your having thrown yourself at a man like Drakon Lyonedes.'

'I did not throw myself at him!' Gemini protested.

'Liar!' Angela straightened abruptly, her eyes once again glittering. 'I always knew you didn't like me, Gemini—and, believe me, the feeling is completely reciprocated. As far as I'm concerned you've always been far too much of a reminder of the perfect first wife that Miles so obviously adored.'

'How could you possibly have been jealous of a dead woman?' Gemini gasped.

'I was never jealous of Rosemary!' Angela glared furiously.

'It sounds distinctly like jealousy to me,' she retorted.

'And what would you know about it, little rich girl?' the other woman demanded. 'You lived in a mansion all your life, doted on by rich and indulgent parents, you owned your own pony, attended private schools, and holidayed in exotic places all over the world several times a year. What would you know about growing up on the twelfth floor of a tenement building in a family of six who had nothing to look forward to but the next dole cheque?'

'I— That was you?'

'Oh, yes,' Angela sneered. 'Until I reached sixteen and was old enough to break my ties with my family in order to reinvent myself and use the one asset I have— my body and the way that I look. Of course I had to put up with the pawing of a succession of wealthy old men, but it was all worth it when I finally persuaded the wealthiest one into marrying me.'

Gemini went deathly white at these revelations. 'You told my father that your father had gambled away your family fortune before committing suicide—'

'And he did gamble—probably still does. What little money the government gave us always went to the bookies or on another bottle of whisky to throw down his throat,' Angela said harshly. 'He rarely, if ever, gave my mother enough money to actually *feed* any of us.'

'You told my father that both your parents were dead.'

'I lied,' Angela admitted. 'I've never been back, but as far as I'm aware both my parents are still alive—and no doubt living in exactly the same squalor as always.'

Gemini could perhaps understand what had driven Angela into seducing Miles into marriage now that she knew the truth of the other woman's background—obviously any wealthy man would have done. Could understand and even sympathise with her. What she couldn't accept was the unhappiness that selfishness had caused her disillusioned father before he died…

She took a deep breath. 'I'm sorry if that truly is how you were forced to live as a child—'

'Oh, it's all true,' Angela assured her. 'And you can keep your sympathy for someone who might actually appreciate it. After all, I came out the winner in the end, didn't I?'

Oh, yes, Angela had certainly triumphed. Spectacularly, in fact, with regard to Gemini's father.

'I suppose Drakon Lyonedes was to be your second, even wealthier husband?'

'Why not?' Angela demanded aggressively.

Gemini gave a pained frown. 'Don't you have enough money now, having sold off everything my father left you?'

'I'll *never* have enough money,' the older woman said with hard determination.

'And never care who you have to trample over in order to get it, apparently,' Gemini said dully.

'That's rich, coming from you!' Angela jeered.

'You're still so desperate to own Bartholomew House that you would even stoop to trying to seduce Drakon yourself to get it!'

Gemini felt ill. In fact she thought she might actually be sick if she had to stand and listen to this woman for too much longer. 'Considering your claim that *you're* involved with Drakon, I'm surprised you believe he could be seduced—by me or any other woman.'

'I believe I said you had *tried* to seduce him,' Angela scoffed. 'I'm sure you very quickly learnt that a man like Drakon requires a woman who's a little more adventurous and experienced than a mere baby like you!'

Just thinking of Drakon and Angela together intimately, after the passionate way he had kissed her in the lift four days ago, brought on another wave of nausea. She swallowed hard. 'I'm afraid I'm going to have to ask you to leave after all.'

'I'm not going anywhere until I've made it perfectly clear to you that Bartholomew House—and Drakon—will never be yours!' Angela announced.

Gemini gave a slow and disbelieving shake of her head. 'What on earth could a man like Drakon possibly see in someone like *you*?'

Those blue eyes flashed angrily. 'Oh, climb down off your alabaster pedestal, Gemini. If you haven't realised it yet, your own pathetic attempt to seduce Drakon makes you exactly like me!'

Gemini closed her eyes and gave a shudder of distaste. 'God, I hope not.'

'Offends your naive little sensibilities, does it?' Angela taunted.

'Everything about you offends my sensibilities,' Gemini shot back.

'Why, you little—'

'I think not,' interrupted a dangerously soft voice that Gemini instantly recognised.

She opened wide, startled eyes in time to see Drakon take hold of the arm that Angela had raised with the intention of slapping Gemini on the face.

The older woman's face twisted into an ugly mask of hatred as she turned to see who her assailant was. The change that came over Angela's expression then was even more sickening than all that had gone before it. Her eyes softened to a sultry blue as she looked up at Drakon. Her painted red lips curved into an inviting smile, the anger leaving her body as she leant into him.

'Oh, dear, Drakon, I'm afraid you've been caught in the middle of a rather silly argument between two even sillier women,' she murmured throatily.

Gemini felt nausea rise up inside her, and knew she was actually going to be ill after witnessing this sickeningly kittenish display. She only had time to gasp 'Excuse me!' before she brushed past Drakon, heading for the stairs and the privacy of the bathroom in her apartment above the shop.

CHAPTER SEVEN

DRAKON took one look at Gemini collapsed on the floor beside the toilet in the bathroom of her apartment, her face a deathly clammy white after obviously having been violently ill, before striding over to the sink and dampening a flannel with cold water. He went down on his knees beside her to begin bathing her face.

Gemini pushed the flannel away, her eyes a deep and pained sea-green. 'What are you doing?'

He raised dark brows as he sat back on his heels. 'I believe I am endeavouring to make you feel better.'

She gave a humourless smile. 'I'm afraid it's going to take a lot more than the application of a cold flannel to my forehead to succeed in doing that!'

'Gemini—'

'Would you please just go away, Drakon?' She avoided looking at him directly as she reached up and self-consciously flushed the toilet for a second time before lowering the lid and using it as leverage to rise shakily to her feet. 'It's bad enough that I allowed that woman to upset me enough to actually make me physically sick, without the added humiliation of having you witness it,' she muttered, and she picked up her toothbrush and toothpaste and left the bathroom without so much as a second glance in his direction.

Drakon rose slowly to his feet and threw the damp flannel back into the sink. He concentrated on drawing in deep, controlling breaths in an attempt to dampen down the worst of his own anger at the scene he had walked in on a few minutes ago. His hands clenched into fists at his sides as he fought the need to slam one of them into the mirror inset into the wall over the sink.

Following the veiled insights Gemini had given him into Angela Bartholomew's true nature, he had expected the older woman to come straight to the florist's shop and confront Gemini. But, even knowing that, Drakon hadn't been prepared for the scene of violence he had walked in on earlier.

Or his own reaction to it…

A haze of red had literally passed in front of his eyes on seeing Angela's hand raised with the obvious intention of striking Gemini, and for the first time in his life Drakon had actually felt himself tempted into using violence against a woman.

He hadn't done so, of course. That would have been totally against his nature, as well as his parents' teachings. But it had taken every ounce of his self-control not to shake Angela until her perfectly straight white teeth rattled in her vicious head!

Instead he had taken a tight hold of the woman's arm and escorted her from the shop, closing the door firmly behind her before informing Gemini's wide-eyed assistant that her employer was indisposed and probably wouldn't be downstairs again for the rest of the day.

Coming up the stairs to Gemini's apartment and finding her collapsed on the floor of the bathroom, and then having his offer of assistance totally rejected by her, had brought a return of that furious red haze.

So much so that Drakon knew he still didn't have his emotions completely back under iron control when he went in search of her.

Gemini looked up warily as Drakon joined her in the sitting room. She had already hurried into the kitchen and washed her face and cleaned her teeth, but still felt mortified by the scene he had witnessed downstairs, as well as her own physical and embarrassing reaction to it.

But she was even angrier with Drakon for having been the real cause of Angela's vehemence. 'What are you doing here, Drakon?' she demanded dully. 'Isn't it enough that I've had to listen to your mistress insult both my father and myself this afternoon, without having to now suffer your company, too?'

A nerve pulsed in his tightly clenched jaw. Those black eyes glittered darkly. 'I believe I assured you last week that that woman is not, and never will be, my mistress,' he bit out harshly.

Gemini gave a disbelieving snort as she stood beside the unlit fireplace. 'Have you told *her* that?'

'I have no need to tell a woman such as her something she is already only too well aware of,' he said arrogantly.

'Could we please stop the lies?' Gemini pushed the length of her hair back from the paleness of her face. 'We both know that Angela only came here at all today because *you* told her I'd seen you last week.'

That nerve in his jaw pulsed even harder. 'Markos was the one to tell her about that.'

She looked stunned. 'What?'

Drakon sighed at her look of hurt disbelief. 'In self-defence. He had no idea of the trouble it would cause when he did so.'

Gemini stared across at him incredulously. 'You really expect me to believe that?'

He rose up to his full height, appearing every inch the arrogant billionaire industrialist he was in one of his expensively tailored dark suits, pale grey silk shirt, and a darker grey silk tie. The darkness of his hair looked as if it had received a trim since the last time she had seen him.

'I am no more in the habit of lying than you have assured me you are,' he told her coldly.

'I just find it a little hard to believe that Markos needed to tell Angela anything out of self-defence,' she said sceptically.

Drakon looked slightly uncomfortable. 'Apparently she had just propositioned him. Markos was so taken aback by the suggestion that he fell back on his brief acquaintance with you in order to change the subject.'

The first part of that statement sounded a lot like the Angela Gemini now knew far better than she'd ever wished to. It was the second part of the statement that sounded so improbable. 'Your cousin implied that he and I are involved in an attempt to deflect Angela's interest in him?'

Drakon's jaw tightened. 'I believe Markos might have implied that it is you and I who are involved, and that he is also acquainted with you.'

That would certainly explain the arrival of the wrathful Angela. 'And exactly how did he think telling her something like that was going to succeed in saving him from what I'm sure was Angela's less than subtle proposition?'

'Markos obviously had no idea of the animosity with which Angela regards you.' Drakon's nostrils flared. 'Apparently I was her real target, and Markos only second choice. I believe he merely hoped to distract even those second-hand attentions by drawing attention to our own acquaintance.'

Gemini stared at Drakon wordlessly for several seconds. The directness of that unwavering dark gaze challenged her to continue disbelieving him. Which she found she couldn't do. The explanation was so ridiculous—and sounded so exactly like something Angela would do—that Gemini couldn't help but believe it.

She felt some of the tension leave her body as she gave a rueful sigh. 'Poor Markos.'

'Poor Markos?' Drakon repeated incredulously, knowing that at this moment in time he could cheerfully have pummelled his cousin to a pulp—something he hadn't done since they had been children together—for being the cause of Angela's verbal and physical assault on Gemini.

Gemini nodded. 'I like Markos.'

Drakon noted grimly that she did not say she felt that same liking for him. Not that he could exactly blame her. So far in their acquaintance Gemini had believed him to be involved in an affair with her father's widow, to be responsible for denying her the right to purchase her family home, and to add insult to injury he had then proceeded to make love to her against the wall of a lift in Lyonedes Tower!

No, unfortunately he had no one but himself to blame if Gemini's feelings towards him were more than a little ambivalent.

Drakon looked up as she gave a sudden splutter of laughter. 'Sorry—I was just imagining Markos's panic when Angela propositioned him!' she explained at his questioning look.

'Certainly not his finest hour,' Drakon acknowledged

dryly. 'Although he did at least have the good sense to come to me immediately after she had departed and inform me of what he had done,' he added with a frown. 'I am only sorry I did not arrive soon enough to prevent the unpleasantness of your stepmother's verbal attack.'

'You at least stopped the physical one.' Gemini gave a shrug of her slender shoulders. 'And the verbal stuff was no worse than some of her other outbursts, actually. Better in some ways, because for the first time I actually learnt a little of what motivates her.' She grimaced. 'Not a pretty story, I'm afraid.'

And not one she intended sharing with him either, Drakon guessed. Not that he had any wish to know anything more of Angela, or the reasons she behaved in the way she did. His only concern was Gemini—not the unpleasant woman whom her father had married.

'What did she say to make you physically ill?'

She was very pale still, but even so Drakon couldn't help but appreciate the way the colour of Gemini's short-sleeved blouse perfectly matched the colour of her eyes, making her hair appear even more white-gold. Black jeans fitted smoothly over her bottom and thighs; her bare feet were thrust into flat, open-toed sandals.

Gemini sobered. She was very aware that it was the shock of thinking Drakon was involved with Angela after all, and then his unexpected arrival so quickly after Angela—which at the time had only seemed to confirm his involvement—that had caused her to be so violently ill.

The question was, *why* had it?

She had thought about Drakon a lot these past four days—of their time together in the lift, of her own loss of control—so maybe it had been the thought of his having discussed any of that with Angela which had made her feel so ill? Although if that had really been the case she had no doubt that Angela would have taken great pleasure in telling her so!

'I told you—nothing worse than usual.' Gemini gave a dismissive shake of her head. 'Shouldn't you have flown back to New York by now?'

He glanced down at the plain gold watch on his tanned wrist. 'I was scheduled to leave for the airport an hour ago, yes,' he admitted, before shrugging broad shoulders as he saw her surprised expression. 'I thought it more important that I come here instead, to help you deal with your stepmother,' he explained.

Gemini felt a warm glow inside at the thought of Drakon having changed his arrangements out of concern for her. 'That really was very kind of you,' she murmured huskily. 'Perhaps you'll be able to book another flight later today?'

He smiled tightly. 'It is of no matter; the Lyonedes jet will fly whenever I instruct it to do so.'

'Of course it will.' She nodded ruefully. Silly her—of *course* there was a Lyonedes jet! Her father had been extremely wealthy, but she knew the Lyonedes family were rich beyond her imagining. Hence Angela's obvious interest in ensnaring one of them for herself... 'What on earth did you say to Angela to finally get her to go?' she prompted curiously.

Drakon's top lip curled with distaste as he recalled the unpleasantness of that conversation—the details of which he had no intention of sharing with Gemini. But it had left Drakon feeling it might be of benefit to all concerned if he were to have further investigations made in regard to Angela Bartholomew. If for no other reason than that Lyonedes Enterprises was about to complete an important and costly business transaction with a woman who could not be trusted.

Except Drakon knew there was another, equally important reason for his concern about Angela. And that reason was standing across the room from him.

He'd had every intention of returning to New York this evening—of putting Gemini Bartholomew and the desire that had blazed so hotly between them the previous week firmly from his mind. But now that he had seen her again he knew he no longer felt any inclination to leave England—either today or tomorrow. In fact, he had no desire to leave England until he was reassured that this matter between Gemini and her stepmother had been settled.

And it *would* be settled, Drakon inwardly decreed grimly. One way or another. In such a way that would ensure Gemini was no longer in danger from Angela's viciousness.

'I merely told her that it was time for her to leave,' he answered economically, having no intention of boring Gemini with the truth of her stepmother's flirtatious manner—almost as if he had not witnessed the viciousness of her attack on Gemini!—or the fact that she had dared to invite him out to dinner this evening. It was an invitation Drakon had left the other woman in absolutely no doubt he would refuse—along with any others she might care to make in the future.

The sneering remarks she had made about Gemini following that refusal had been enough to alert Drakon anew concerning Gemini's safety...

'Are you free for dinner this evening?'

Gemini had been lost in thought during Drakon's lengthy silence, but now she looked across at him sharply. 'You're inviting me to have dinner with you again?'

He nodded briskly. 'It is obvious that we need to discuss the continuing problem of your stepmother further, and as I will no longer be flying back to New York today—'

'You won't?' Gemini blinked owlishly, not sure whether that lurch in her stomach was due to a residual nausea from earlier or if it was solely to do with the fact that Drakon apparently wasn't returning to New York today as planned, and had actually invited her out to dinner with him this evening!

It was an invitation she knew she shouldn't accept...

Couldn't accept.

Not when she had spent the past four days telling herself that her heated response to this man had been just a figment of her imagination. An overreaction to everything else that was going on in her life at the moment.

She'd only had to look at Drakon again to know she had been fooling herself...

This man—the way he looked, the aura of power he wore like a mantle about those broad and muscular shoulders—appealed to Gemini on a level she had never experienced before. He somehow made her feel safe, protected, while at the same time being aware that Drakon himself was the biggest danger of all to her. Physically and possibly emotionally as well...

'No. I—' Drakon broke off as a knock sounded on the internal door of the apartment. 'That's probably your assistant. I instructed her to let you know when she was ready to lock up for the day.' He shrugged as Gemini raised her brows.

Yes, Drakon Lyonedes was a man she knew she

should beware of—for more reasons than the obvious one of finding him so mouthwateringly attractive. Left unchecked, he was more than capable of taking over her life if he chose to do so—and was certainly arrogant enough.

'You—' It was Gemini's turn to break off as a mobile phone began to ring. It had to be Drakon's, because the ringtone of hers was one of her favourite songs rather than a normal ringtone like this. 'That's probably Markos, checking to see if you arrived here in time to save me from the clutches of my evil stepmother!' she guessed dryly.

'This situation is not in the least amusing, Gemini.' Dark brows lowered over those coal-black eyes as he removed a mobile phone from the breast pocket of his tailored jacket. 'And I believe my cousin knows me well enough to know I will most certainly have saved you— if indeed you needed saving,' he declared, before taking the call. 'Yes, Markos,' he said, at the same time giving Gemini a small inclination of his head in acknowledgement of her correct guess as to the identity of the caller.

Gemini decided to leave him to the privacy of his call and left the room to answer the door to Jo, reassuring her assistant that she was fine before accompanying her down the stairs to close the blinds and lock the door behind her as she left for the day.

Leaving Gemini completely alone with Drakon…

She lingered downstairs in the shop for several minutes after Jo had gone on her way, restlessly tidying where no tidying was necessary as she thought over Drakon's invitation to dinner this evening. So that they might discuss the problem of Angela further, he had said. Although quite what that meant she had no idea. It was now more than obvious to her that Angela's dislike of her wasn't necessarily personal but was directed towards what Gemini represented. An inborn resentment that she doubted any amount of talking between herself and Drakon would succeed in changing.

Which was reason enough for her to turn down his dinner invitation, surely?

If she wanted to turn it down...

She had total recall of her visit to Lyonedes Tower. Of Drakon's cool arrogance. His remorseless power. Most telling of all, she clearly remembered what it had felt like to have those chiselled lips and those long elegant hands on her body as he made love to her in the lift.

Which was precisely why she shouldn't even *think* about agreeing to have dinner with him again this evening.

'What are you doing alone down here in the darkness?'

Gemini turned sharply to face Drakon, instantly noting how the width of his shoulders almost filled the doorway leading out to the stairs of her apartment. Immediately she was reminded of just how tautly muscled his chest and shoulders had felt beneath her hands...

Not a good memory to have when she was still debating whether or not it would be sensible, even sane on her part, to spend another evening with him!

'Just tidying up,' she said lightly. 'Are you ready to leave now?' she added hopefully.

Drakon looked across at her speculatively. The blinds that had been pulled down over the windows shrouded the shop in half-light, making it impossible for him to see her clearly—although he thought he could make out two bright wings of heated colour in those ivory cheeks.

She also seemed slightly nervous and she avoided meeting his gaze.

'You are not recovered enough to go out to dinner this evening,' he said slowly.

'I—'

'Perhaps you would prefer it if we were to remain here and I prepared something for us to eat?' Drakon suggested swiftly when he sensed she was about to use her earlier indisposition as a way of refusing to have dinner with him. A refusal he had no intention of accepting...

Her eyes widened as she gave a disbelieving huff of laughter. 'You can cook, too?'

'Of course.'

Of course he could cook, Gemini chided herself derisively; he was a man who gave the impression that he could do absolutely anything he chose to. 'Well?' she asked in a reminder of the conversation they'd had the previous week when she'd asked if he played the piano in his apartment.

'Passably.' His mouth curved into a wry smile in acknowledgement of that conversation.

Gemini laughed. 'In that case you can certainly cook for me some time.'

He quirked dark brows. 'But not this evening?'

She shrugged. 'I really don't see that there would be any point. Angela is—well, Angela.' She grimaced. 'And whatever bee she currently has in her bonnet over me will no doubt pass when she gets some other multi-billionaire in her matrimonial sights.'

Drakon frowned. 'Did you really believe earlier that I was involved with her in a personal way?'

Yes, briefly, she *had* once again believed that. How could she have thought anything else when the other

woman had appeared here like an avenging angel and
accused Gemini of trying to seduce Drakon?

Gemini shrugged again. 'It really doesn't matter what
I do or don't believe on that subject, does it?'

'Oh, but it does,' Drakon murmured as he stepped
further into the shadows. 'To me it matters very much.'

Gemini swallowed hard as she watched him approach
with lithe, purposeful strides, only coming to a halt
when he stood mere inches away from her. 'I—it's all
been sorted out now, so no real harm done,' she dismissed nervously.

He raised an eyebrow. 'Surely that is for me to say,
and not you?'

She drew in a deep breath and let it out slowly. 'Stop
making such a big thing out of it, Drakon.'

'But it *is* a big thing to have one's word doubted, is
it not?' he pressed softly.

Gemini gave him an irritated frown. 'You want me
to apologise for ever having doubted you? Is that it?'

Those sculptured lips curved in a smile. 'That would
certainly be a start, yes.'

'A start?' she repeated warily, not sure she was comfortable with the way Drakon stood so overpoweringly
close to her. Or with the direction this conversation appeared to be going in.

'A start,' he echoed huskily as he closed the small
distance between them, his hands moving up to lightly
grasp the tops of her arms as his head began to lower
towards hers.

Yes, their conversation was going in exactly the direction Gemini had thought it might!

CHAPTER EIGHT

She swallowed hard. 'Drakon—'

'Gemini…' he murmured throatily, his breath a warm caress across her lips.

She felt trapped, very like a rabbit caught in the glare of the headlights of a car, as she continued to stare up at him in the semi-darkness and felt the unmistakable pull of physical attraction. 'This isn't a good idea at all.'

Those dark eyes glittered. 'I disagree.'

Gemini blinked. 'You do?'

'Oh, yes,' Drakon muttered, and her nearness, the heady seduction of her perfume, took over all of his senses as he finally claimed her lips with his own.

He had thought often of doing this again, he realised as her lips parted, yielded to his, and he drew her fully into his arms to deepen the kiss. Taking. Possessing. His hands moved restlessly, searchingly over the sweet curves of her back and the smooth roundness of her bottom, pulling her into him and making her fully aware of the hard pulse of his arousal.

Yes, he had thought of this many times these past four days. Yearned for this. Ached for it.

There was no room for other thoughts now except to indulge those senses. No time for gentleness as his tongue plundered the sweetness of her mouth until he knew every warm and delicious inch. The warm swell of her breasts was crushed against the hardness of his chest, her thighs were hot against him, and the air filled with the raggedness of their breathing and their low moans of pleasure.

To Gemini it was as if no time at all had passed since Drakon had last made love to her. The passion was instant—the need, the aching pleasure even more so. She gasped as his fingers touched her skin beneath her blouse seconds before his hand cupped the lace of her bra, groaning in her throat as her nipple rubbed against the heat of his palm.

He moved back slightly to unbutton her blouse and reveal those lace-cupped breasts to his glittering black gaze before he expertly removed the skimpy item of lingerie and let it fall on the floor, along with her blouse.

Gemini slid the jacket from his shoulders and down his arms before dropping it onto the floor to join her discarded clothing, allowing the briefest moment of humour as she imagined the horror of Drakon's tailor at her cavalier treatment of a jacket that she was sure had cost thousands of dollars.

But it was only the briefest of thoughts before Gemini released the knot of his tie and tossed it aside, unfastening the buttons of the white silk shirt and revealing the muscled perfection of his olive-skinned chest. The shirt met the same fate as his jacket, and her breath caught in her throat as she was finally able to touch the glorious contours of his bared flesh.

Steel encased in velvet...

Gemini could feel the play of muscles beneath that velvet warmth as Drakon's mouth once again claimed hers, and she moved her arms about his waist to caress the long length of his naked back, down over the tautness of his fabric-covered buttocks and then up along the length of his spine.

He dragged his lips from hers to taste the delicate skin of her throat, the top swell of her breasts, before moving lower, capturing the hard nub of her nipple and drawing it into the heat of his mouth.

She gasped, her bare back against the brick wall as Drakon curled his fingers about her thighs and lifted her up and into him until her legs were about his waist. Her fingers became entangled in the darkness of his hair and pleasure coursed through her as she felt the hard throb of his arousal against her core.

That pleasure pooled between her thighs in a warm rush of moisture as he began to move slowly against her. At the same time his hand moved to cup her other breast, sliding a rhythmic thumb again and again over that second throbbing peak until she wanted to die from the arousing onslaught of his clever lips and hands and fingers.

Gemini could only cling to the dampness of Drakon's bare shoulders as she felt herself spiralling high, ever higher. He continued pleasuring her breasts at the same time as his throbbing shaft rubbed against that sensitised nub between her thighs. Her breath was coming in short and painful gasps as she hurtled closer and closer towards a release that filled her with a longing to pull Drakon closer at the same time as a fear of completely losing control of her senses urged her to push him away.

Drakon seemed to sense that confusion in her. His eyes were dark and glittering as he slowly released his mouth from her breast and looked up at her. 'I'm not hurting you, am I?'

'God, no!' she choked out, trembling, shaking from the force of her own arousal.

An arousal that he seemed to incite in her at will...

An arousal that was rapidly fading, to be replaced by embarrassment as she realised exactly what they were doing—and where!

'I just—I'm finding all of this a bit overwhelming, Drakon. Making love for the first time was somehow always more...romantic in my imaginings.' She made an attempt at humour as she forced her knees to relax their death grip about his waist, her legs feeling slightly shaky as she allowed her feet to slide down to the concrete floor.

He blinked. 'Sorry?'

'It's silly, I know,' she gabbled. 'But I'd always thought that the first time I made love it would at least be in a huge feather bed—maybe even a four-poster.'

'A four-poster bed?'

'Mmm. With curtains blowing in a gentle breeze,' Gemini mused as the idea of making love with Drakon in such a romantic setting began to take flight.

'I beg your pardon?'

'And maybe rose petals scattered about the room,' she continued dreamily. 'Don't you think that would be romantic, Drakon?'

'Undoubtedly,' he rasped.

Gemini snapped out of her romantic musings as she became aware of the wariness in his tone. And not just wariness, but utter disbelief.

And a healthy dose of shock!

No doubt it *was* a shock for him to realise that the spoilt and pampered daughter of Miles Bartholomew was a twenty-seven-year-old virgin...

What on earth had she been thinking, drivelling on like that in front of a man like him?

Her cheeks burned hotly. 'What did you imagine,

Drakon?' Her embarrassment deepened as she picked up her blouse and quickly put it on over her bare breasts. 'Did you think that I make a habit of behaving in this uninhibited way with every man I meet?'

His jaw tightened. 'Not every man, no.'

'Just the rich and powerful ones?'

A scowl darkened his brow. 'Gemini—'

'If you really thought that, then I'm afraid you have me confused with my stepmother,' she cut in before he could answer her.

'I know exactly who and what you are, Gemini,' he grated.

The rustle of clothing behind her told her that Drakon had probably pulled his shirt back on at least. The shirt she had only minutes ago unbuttoned before throwing on the floor!

What was it about this man in particular that made her behave so completely out of character? Gemini barely recognised the wanton she became every time Drakon took her in his arms.

And a drivelling, romantic idiot too, apparently!

Something a man like him would certainly be repelled by.

Gemini kept her back towards him and moved to the safety of the other side of the shop before turning. Only the whiteness of Drakon's shirt was visible where he still stood in the shadows. She licked her lips. 'Don't misunderstand me, Drakon. I'm really very grateful for the help you gave me earlier in getting rid of Angela, but not grateful enough to—'

'I strongly advise that you don't insult me by finishing that sentence,' he warned, the tone of his voice dangerously soft.

Gemini shivered as she felt the chill of his warning

down the length of her spine. A warning she would be
insane not to heed! 'I don't mean to insult you—'

'No?' he rasped as he bent down to pick his jacket
and tie up from the floor.

'No,' she reiterated wearily. 'That's the last thing I
want to do when you've been so…kind.' She shrugged.
'It's just been one hell of a day. Emotions are running
high, and I really think it would be best if you just left
now.'

Drakon agreed with the logic of her reasoning. At
least he would have agreed with it if he could have
thought logically at all. As it was, he was still reeling
from the knowledge that, although Gemini was a so-
phisticated young woman in her late twenties, she was
a physically inexperienced one.

How was such a thing possible in this day and age?
Especially for a beautiful young woman whose father's
wealth would have ensured she had lived her life in
privilege and self-indulgence? When her late teens and
early twenties would have been spent socialising with
men of wealth and experience? When Gemini's own
stepmother was an acknowledged seductress?

But perhaps Gemini's contempt for the latter was the
very reason she had chosen a completely different path
for herself?

Whatever the explanation for her physical innocence,
Drakon was stunned by it. Stunned and at the same time
wary. He had been sexually active for more than twenty
years now, and never in all his thirty-six years had he
made love to an innocent. As much as he still wanted
and desired Gemini—and it seemed he had only to look
at her to want her—he had no intention of complicating
his own life or hers by becoming her very first lover.

His movements were measured, deliberate, as he

shrugged back into his jacket and then neatly folded his tie and placed it in one of his pockets before looking across at Gemini once more. 'After witnessing her behaviour earlier, I don't believe for a moment that you have seen the last of your stepmother,' he remarked with obvious distaste.

Gemini didn't think so either; she knew her stepmother far too well to ever believe that. Angela seemed to have set her sights on ensnaring one of the Lyonedes men as her next husband—preferably Drakon—and, as Gemini knew only too well, the older woman wasn't easily deterred once she had set her mind on making a conquest.

Knowing of Gemini's acquaintance with both men— these encounters with Drakon were far too physically volatile for her ever to think of them as friends—was surely only guaranteed to make Angela even more determined to capture one of the Lyonedes cousins. If only out of spite towards Gemini.

She shrugged ruefully. 'As long as you and Markos stay well away from her in future there shouldn't be a problem.'

Drakon gave a humourless smile. 'That may be a little difficult when we are in the middle of a business transaction with her.'

Gemini stiffened at this reminder that Lyonedes Enterprises was in the process of purchasing her family home from Angela. 'I believe you walked yourself into that particular situation,' she said unsympathetically.

'Indeed,' he accepted dryly. 'And it is a situation I am more than capable of dealing with. But I would advise that you do everything in your power to avoid any further confrontation with her.'

Gemini looked him directly in the eyes. 'Maybe you should just give her what she wants and take her to bed?'

Drakon drew in a harsh breath at the very thought of having a sexual relationship with the avaricious widow. Not that she was unattractive—if a man did not mind knowing her interest was mainly in his bank balance!

Which, he acknowledged, was something that had never particularly bothered him before. Indeed, it was the reason he had become so cynical and jaded about ever finding a woman who might love him for himself, and whom he could love in return. Years of having women attracted to the Lyonedes name and his excessive wealth had resulted in unemotional and consequently fleeting relationships with women.

His continued attraction to Gemini—a young woman whom he now knew was neither avaricious nor experienced—was unsettling to say the least.

He eyed her dispassionately and nodded abruptly. 'I will give your suggestion all the consideration it deserves.' Which, as far as he was concerned, was none whatsoever.

Gemini recoiled as if Drakon had physically struck her. Which, in a way, he had.

For the past four years she had stood back and watched as dozens of men had fallen prey to the allure of Angela's voluptuous beauty—her own father included—and to think of Drakon, a man whose attraction she seemed unable to resist herself, becoming another one of Angela's conquests brought a return of Gemini's earlier nausea.

She frowned. 'Obviously you must do what you think best…'

Those almost black eyes glittered coldly. 'I invariably do,' he rasped harshly.

Yes, she had no doubt that he was a man who answered to no one for any of his actions. And really she had brought this current situation on herself. Out of self-defence and confusion over her attraction towards Drakon, maybe, but nevertheless she had instigated this particular conversation.

'Thank you once again for your help earlier.'

'You're welcome.' He gave a brief inclination of his head.

'No doubt you'll be returning to New York now?'

Drakon had decided earlier that to leave England before the issue of Angela Bartholomew was settled to his satisfaction would be an error of judgement on his part. But this time spent with Gemini, when he had once again found himself unable to resist making love to her, only to learn that she was an innocent, told him that it would perhaps be an even bigger error of judgement on his part if he were to remain. Only perhaps? It could become a catastrophic error of judgement for both of them if he were to remain in England at this present time!

'No doubt,' he replied noncommittally as he strolled over and opened the shop door. 'Lock the door behind me.'

Gemini glared at his autocratic back as she followed him. 'I have every intention of doing so.'

Drakon looked down at her wordlessly for several long seconds before sighing. 'Don't hesitate to call on Markos if it should become necessary.'

Call on Markos, not him, she noted heavily as she shut and secured the door after Drakon left. He couldn't have told her any more plainly that their own brief association, whatever it might have been, was very definitely over as far as he was concerned.

Drakon waited only long enough to hear Gemini lock the door behind him before taking his mobile out of his pocket and pressing a quick-dial button as he walked the short distance to where he had parked his car earlier.

'Have Max arrange for a twenty-four-hour watch to be kept on Gemini,' he instructed economically when his cousin answered the call on only the second ring. 'And first thing in the morning have him do a thorough check on Angela Bartholomew,' he added grimly before Markos had time to respond to that first instruction. 'I also want him to look into the possibility of Miles Bartholomew having drawn up a will dated later than the one that was presented for probate.' He unlocked and opened the door of the Mercedes and slid into the leather seat behind the wheel. 'A will that may have left Bartholomew House to his daughter rather than his wife.'

'Do you think that's a possibility?'

'After today, I think Angela is a woman capable of doing anything that is in her own best interests.'

'Including illegally suppressing her husband's will?'

'Including that, yes,' Drakon confirmed grimly.

'Hell!' Markos groaned heavily. 'That could leave Lyonedes Enterprises in one almighty legal tangle.'

It would also, if it existed, leave Gemini in a position of great vulnerability… 'Yes,' he agreed tersely.

'And where will you will be while I'm instructing Max to do these things?' Markos prompted curiously.

Drakon glanced across at the closed and shuttered flower shop that Gemini owned and ran. His gaze was drawn upwards to where a light had come on in what he now knew to be the sitting room of her apartment. 'I have decided to leave for New York this evening after all.'

'Really?' Markos sounded surprised.

'Really,' Drakon echoed dryly. There was no reason for him to return to Lyonedes Tower; he rarely carried luggage with him anyway, as he kept a full wardrobe of clothes in both his New York apartment and the one here in London.

'But Gemini is okay?'

He frowned his irritation at his cousin's obvious concern. 'She appeared to be perfectly well when I left her two minutes ago,' he snapped.

'And her stepmother?'

'Is a bitch from hell, and we should never have entered into a business transaction with her,' Drakon felt no hesitation in announcing harshly.

There was a brief pause before Markos spoke again. 'I'll talk to Max straight away.'

'Do that.'

Drakon ended the call as abruptly as he had started it. His second call to the pilot of the Lyonedes jet was even briefer as he sat and watched Gemini's shadowy outline inside her apartment as she moved to pull the curtains across the two windows that faced down onto the street.

He was still sitting there in the silence of the Mercedes fifteen minutes later when a black Range Rover, with Max himself seated behind the wheel, pulled into the parking space behind. He turned in his seat, and the two men nodded brief acknowledgement of each other before Drakon started his engine and drove away.

* * *

'Well!' Gemini huffed indignantly as she slowly replaced the telephone receiver on its cradle.

'Problems?' Jo looked across at her curiously as she came to collect her jacket from the office of the shop in preparation for leaving for her lunch break on what was turning out to be a very busy Friday.

Drakon Lyonedes had been a problem before Gemini had even met him! And he had become even more of one—for totally different reasons—since she had first forced herself into his presence. Had that really only been a week ago? It somehow seemed so much longer.

Gemini still inwardly cringed every time she thought about the last time she had seen him three days ago.

Considering how the time usually flew by when she was at work, it had been a surprisingly long three days. Three days during which Drakon had completely disappeared from her life.

No, not completely…

She had slept badly the night after he'd left her so abruptly. Not because she had wasted any more of her time thinking about that awful scene with Angela, but because she hadn't been able to stop thinking about Drakon and her response to him. Consequently it had taken her until late the following morning to notice the black Range Rover parked just down the street from the flower shop, and several more hours to realise that Max Stanford was seated behind the wheel, his steely gaze fixed unwaveringly on the flower shop. On her?

Gemini had decided she was being paranoid, and the Range Rover had disappeared when she'd gone out later that morning to buy her lunch from the deli two doors down the street. And then she had realised that another black car had taken the place of the Range Rover, and the man sitting inside seemed to be watching her from behind concealing sunglasses. By the time she'd shut up shop for the night the black Range Rover and Max were back, and the other car and its driver had disappeared.

Still feeling ever so slightly paranoid, Gemini had nevertheless felt no hesitation in walking over to the Range Rover and tapping on the window to ask an obviously less than pleased Max exactly what he was doing, parked outside her shop. His curt explanation had been enough to send Gemini hurrying back inside to put a call straight through to Markos.

Charming and roguish as ever, Markos had assured her that he was simply carrying out his cousin's instructions, and that Max, or one of his security team, was to remain as her protection until Drakon told him otherwise.

Gemini had been stunned. And not a little annoyed. She accepted that Angela had been verbally abusive the last time the two women had spoken, and that Drakon had walked in on that heated scene just in time to prevent her stepmother from actually hitting her, but surely he didn't imagine Angela would actually try to harm her?

That question had unfortunately remained unanswered, because Gemini's efforts to contact Drakon in New York had proved as difficult as contacting him at Lyonedes Tower had been the previous week. She had managed to get as far as talking to his personal assistant this time, only to be informed that Mr Lyonedes was unavailable. Nor had Drakon bothered to return her call.

She had now received a telephone call from that same personal assistant, telling her that, 'Mr Lyonedes has instructed me to inform you that he will be arriving in

England later today and will be calling on you at your apartment at eight o'clock this evening.' It just added insult to injury. Gemini had a good mind to make sure she was nowhere near her apartment at eight o'clock tonight!

Although she accepted that wasn't likely to achieve very much when the current watchdog parked outside would no doubt tell Drakon exactly where she had gone. Still, it was the principle of the thing that mattered; damn it, Drakon couldn't just walk in and out of her life and take charge whenever he felt like it! Well…apparently he could. But that didn't mean that she had to make it at all easy for him.

She looked up now and smiled reassuringly at Jo. 'It's nothing I can't handle,' she assured her assistant firmly.

At least Gemini sincerely hoped she *could* handle seeing Drakon again…

CHAPTER NINE

'ARE you expecting someone to join you?'

Gemini had been aware of Drakon the moment he entered her favourite Italian restaurant. Just as she had been aware of the female interest directed towards him as he inexorably made his way across that restaurant to where she sat at a table in one of the more private booths at the back of the happily noisy and crowded room. A table set for two.

Her own heart had skipped a beat at how dark and dangerously attractive Drakon looked this evening, in a casual black silk shirt, unbuttoned at the throat, and black trousers tailored to the long length of his legs. The darkness of his hair was slightly tousled and damp, as if he had recently taken a shower. Which he probably had, she accepted, if he had only flown in from New York a few hours ago.

She put down her glass of Chianti to lean back against the leather bench seat. She looked up and smiled at him. 'Yes, I'm expecting someone to join me,' she confirmed lightly.

Drakon looked more than a little irritated. 'Did my assistant not telephone you earlier to tell you I would be calling at your apartment this evening?'

'Oh, yes, he telephoned me,' Gemini said blandly.

'Then—'

'Obviously I had plans for this evening other than sitting at home waiting for the great Drakon Lyonedes to grace me with his magnificent presence,' she continued as though he hadn't spoken.

He would have to be blind not to notice the way those sea-green eyes flashed with temper. And unfortunately he wasn't in the least visually impaired where Gemini Bartholomew was concerned! 'You are annoyed that I asked my assistant to telephone you.' It was a statement not a question.

'How astute of you, Drakon!' she came back with saccharine sweetness.

If anything Gemini looked more beautiful this evening than when Drakon had last seen her: those sparkling eyes were surrounded by long dark lashes, colour highlighted her cheeks, the fullness of her lips was glossed peach, and her hair was a silky white-blonde curtain about her slender shoulders. The fitted cotton sweater she wore was the same sea-green colour as her eyes, and a short black skirt revealed the length of her legs.

Drakon's mouth thinned as he realised he was not at all pleased to know she had dressed like that for the pleasure of another man. 'Are you saying you would rather I had telephoned and spoken to you personally before I left New York?' he queried.

Her eyes once more glowed with temper. 'I'm saying I would rather you had bothered to return my call two days ago, or at the very least telephoned me yesterday and *asked* if it was convenient for us to meet this evening, rather than just having your assistant call and *tell* me that we were!'

Yes, that would have been the more acceptable, the

more polite way of doing things, Drakon acknowledged impatiently. Except he had not been feeling in the least polite—either yesterday or any of the other days he had been back in New York. Because of this woman. Because he had not been able to stop thinking about Gemini and the last time the two of them had been together. Or how much he wished to see her and be with her again…

That knowledge alone had been enough to make his temper and mood unpredictable at best these past three days, and volatile at worst. Nor, he acknowledged irritably, had he been in the least sure of how much she would have welcomed the call if he had been the one to telephone today…

Drakon had accepted long ago that he was a man of strong sexual appetites, but also a man who rarely if ever thought of any of the women he made love to when he was not sharing her body and her bed. Gemini Bartholomew, he had learnt these past few days, was the exception to that rule—and he didn't like it one little bit.

He had found himself thinking of her far too often for comfort since flying back to New York, both at work and during the long evenings spent at his penthouse apartment in Manhattan. Neither did he have to look far to find the reason for his feelings of frustration where she was concerned.

Gemini's admission of physical innocence…

Drakon had been stunned. It was incredible, unbelievable, that a woman of her beauty and years should still be a virgin. It also put her beyond the reach of his normal casual affairs. Unfortunately that in no way lessened the desire Drakon felt for her…

Just seeing her again, being with her again, was enough to make his body harden with a ferocious desire!

'Oh, for goodness' sake sit down and stop making the place look untidy, Drakon,' she snapped as the waiter arrived at the table and handed her two menus before departing again.

He frowned. 'I thought you said you were waiting for someone.'

'I was,' Gemini said. 'And now he's arrived. I was waiting for you, Drakon,' she admitted as he continued to stare down at her.

His eyes widened. 'Me?'

'I was pretty sure one of your watchdogs would be only too happy to tell you exactly where to find me at eight o'clock this evening,' she told him. 'And, as you very kindly gave me dinner at your apartment last time, I thought the least I could do was buy you dinner at my favourite Italian restaurant this evening. Would you care for a glass of red wine?' She lifted up the bottle of Chianti she had ordered when she arrived and held it poised over the empty wine glass at the place setting opposite her own.

'Thank you,' Drakon accepted quietly as he slid onto the bench seat opposite, more relieved than he cared to consider at the knowledge that Gemini was not spending the evening with another man after all. That she had, in fact, dressed this way for his pleasure. 'I apologise if you found my assistant's telephone call impolite.'

Gemini looked across the table at Drakon from beneath lowered lashes, knowing she was once again slightly overwhelmed by the sheer presence of this man. Even dressed in casual clothes he exuded that aura of power and authority. 'Your assistant was perfectly polite, Drakon—you're the one I consider rude and high-handed in asking him to make the call in the first place.'

Drakon returned her gaze quizzically. 'You don't intend to let me off the hook lightly, do you?'

'Should I?' Gemini deliberately showed none of the inner turmoil she felt at seeing Drakon again as she casually picked up her wine glass and took a sip of the deliciously fruity red wine.

'Probably not.' He shrugged those broad shoulders.

'Definitely not,' she corrected pointedly.

Drakon sighed. 'Very well. I apologise unreservedly, Gemini, for not telephoning you myself and requesting a meeting with you.'

'You're forgiven.' She gave a graciously acknowledging inclination of her head.

'So this is your favourite restaurant...' Drakon looked about them appreciatively, finding the warm and cosy atmosphere of the restaurant also to *his* liking.

There were red-and-white-checked cloths on the twenty or so occupied tables, with candles alight in empty wine bottles on each one, lots of greenery trailing down from above, brightly coloured pictures of Italy adorning the terracotta-coloured walls, and the delicious smells of garlic and Italian sauces coming from the kitchen were enough to make his mouth water.

'Not what you were expecting?'

Drakon's gaze returned across the table to Gemini as he heard the amusement in her voice. Inwardly he acknowledged that nothing about this young woman was what he would have expected from the only daughter of the wealthy and influential Miles Bartholomew. Which, he knew, was becoming a serious problem for him; Gemini was rapidly throwing all his previous experience with women off-balance. Throwing *him* off-balance...

He shrugged as he picked up the menu. 'I'm sure the food here is adequate.'

She gave an indelicate snort. 'The food here is fantastic!'

Drakon perused the extensive menu. 'What would you recommend?'

Gemini studied his bent head, noting the way his hair had started to curl slightly as it dried in the warmth of the restaurant. The sharp angles of his face were softened by the warm glow of candlelight, and the silky dark hair visible at the base of his throat where his shirt was unbuttoned instantly made her remember how that soft pelt went all the way down to his—

'Gemini?'

A blush warmed her cheeks as she raised her startled gaze to meet Drakon's glittering black one. 'Anything,' she answered abruptly. 'All the food here is good.'

Those dark eyes continued to study her for long, timeless seconds. Tense, still seconds, when even the chatter of the other diners faded into the background and there seemed to be only Gemini and Drakon in the room, and she found herself totally unable to look away from that compelling gaze.

Gemini had hoped that if she ever saw Drakon again she would find she had got over whatever madness had possessed her the last time she had seen him—well, the last two times she had seen him! That she would be able to look at him, speak to him, spend time with him and see him for the arrogant, powerful man that he was. And it was impossible *not* to see those things in him. Unfortunately she knew he was also dangerously seductive; he only had to touch her, kiss her, to send her over the edge of self-control. Something that had never, ever happened to her before, but seemed to happen constantly with him. As she'd said, he was extremely dangerous...

She straightened, determined to break the sensual spell that once again threatened to engulf and claim her. 'So, how has your week been?' she asked with brittle brightness.

'Busy.' Drakon put down his menu. 'Yours?'

She shrugged. 'The same.'

'There have been no more visits from your stepmother?'

Gemini gave him a cool look. 'I'm sure Max has duly reported that there haven't.'

Drakon's mouth thinned. 'Markos informed me that you were less than pleased at Max's watchfulness.'

'Did he?' she mused. 'Didn't seem to make much difference to the outcome, did it?'

Drakon sighed heavily. 'Would you rather I had left you completely at the mercy of that woman's vindictiveness?'

'Once again, I would rather you had asked first,' she said pointedly.

He raised dark brows. 'And if I had done so?'

'I would have assured you that it wasn't necessary.' She waved an elegant hand. 'You were the reason Angela went off the deep end in the first place, and with you out of the picture...'

Drakon gave a humourless smile. 'Unless it has escaped your notice, I have returned.'

As if any woman could be unaware of the presence of Drakon Lyonedes! The man only had to enter a room in order to dominate it. A point that was ably demonstrated only seconds later, when Benito came to take

their order and completely deferred to Drakon throughout the entire conversation.

'What?' he prompted when he saw Gemini frowning across the width of the table at him once they were
alone again.

She shook her head. 'You totally ruined my usual
couple of minutes of flirting outrageously with Benito
when he comes to take my order.'

Drakon's brows rose. 'You flirt with the waiter?'

'I flirt outrageously,' she corrected. 'And Benito is
the owner of the restaurant, not the waiter.'

He glanced across to where the dark-haired, handsome young man was passing their order to a shorter,
portly man to take to the kitchen, before resuming his
place behind the desk at the entrance to the restaurant.
'You come to this restaurant because you like to flirt
with the owner?' His gaze was hard and glittering when
he turned it back to Gemini.

'No, I come here because the food is excellent—*and*
I like to flirt with the owner,' Gemini added with a teasing smile.

Drakon failed to see anything in the least amusing
about her obvious attraction to Benito. 'Your usual male
companions must find that very…unflattering.'

'What do you mean by that?' she asked.

Drakon scowled. 'The men you usually bring here
on a date.'

She sat back on the seat, her brows mockingly high.
'I wasn't aware *this* was a date.'

It wasn't. At least it hadn't been Drakon's intention
that it should become one when he had decided he and
Gemini must meet again this evening. And yet the two
of them were sitting together in a cosy Italian restaurant. At a secluded table for two. With a lit candle in

its centre. And an evening of possibilities stretching before them. Yes, it certainly had all of the ingredients of a date, he recognised heavily.

He shrugged. 'For the sake of appearances let us say that it is.'

For the sake of Gemini's sense of self-preservation she would rather say that it wasn't! Admittedly she had been the one to instigate this evening's meeting taking place at a restaurant rather than her apartment, as he had stipulated through his assistant.

But that was the whole point, wasn't it? She had made her own arrangements for the evening because she had resented Drakon's arrogance in issuing that instruction through a third party!

Except she didn't seem to have thought it through as thoroughly as she ought to have done. Hadn't even considered that the two of them sitting here, talking and eating a meal together, would take on all the appearance of a date. Which was a bit late in the day when you considered she'd already allowed him to make love to her. *Twice!*

'I do hope you intend to give poor Max a couple of hours off, at least, while we eat dinner?' she said sweetly.

Drakon instantly recognised her deliberate attempt to remind him exactly why she would never consider their having dinner together as being a date—his arrogant high-handedness in having her watched over by his security team.

'Poor Max?' he queried.

She nodded once their first course had been delivered to the table and the waiter had departed. 'I'm sure you pay him and the rest of your security team well, but even so it must still have been very boring for them to just sit outside my apartment for the past three days and nights.'

Yes, Drakon had read Max's daily reports with interest, noting that Gemini spent her days in her shop and her evenings and nights alone in her apartment. 'You are correct. I do pay them very well,' he said. 'And I believe you very kindly offered Max some variation in your routine when you closed the shop yesterday afternoon.'

She gave a mischievous grin. 'He told you about that?'

Even in reading Max's e-mailed report Drakon had been able to pick up on the older man's discomfort at having to follow Gemini into a large beauty salon, where she had proceeded to have her hair styled, then a manicure and a pedicure, before disappearing into a private room in order to have various parts of her delectable body waxed.

'He may never recover from the experience,' Drakon commented.

Gemini had actually come to like and respect Max Stanford during the past few days—had even invited him into the shop a couple of times for coffee when she'd thought he might be in need of a drink. She just hadn't been able to resist teasing him a little when it came to the usual relaxing way she spent her Thursday afternoons off. Besides which, she had been fully aware of the fact that, as with everything else she had done the past three days, he would report her movements to his employer.

She eyed Drakon quizzically. 'And not you?'

He shrugged those broad shoulders. 'My mother usually spends her Saturday afternoons in the same way, I believe.'

His widowed mother, Gemini knew, had lived alone in Athens since the death of her husband ten years ago. In fact, she knew quite a lot more about Drakon now than she had three days ago; the internet was a marvelous although potentially dangerous thing, offering any amount of information on someone as famous as him.

Such as the extent of his business interests around the world, as well as his extreme wealth. He owned homes in New York, London, Hong Kong, Toronto and Paris, as well as a private island in the Greek Aegean—although how he ever found the time to live in most of those homes was a mystery to her when he obviously worked so hard adding to the Lyonedes millions.

She also knew that he was thirty-six years old. And single. With not so much as a hint of an engagement in his past…

She eyed him curiously now. 'Are you and your mother close?'

'Very,' he said economically.

'And you and Markos are close too?'

'Like brothers,' he confirmed.

'I noticed that.'

Drakon raised dark brows. 'You find it strange that I not only feel affection for my family but also engender a return of that affection?'

'Not in the least,' she dismissed lightly. 'Why would I? I'm sure you're a very attentive son, and the closeness between you and Markos was all too obvious when I saw you together last week.'

The slightly wistful note in Gemini's voice reminded Drakon that her twin brother had died before she'd even had a chance to know him, and that with the death of both of her parents she now had no family of her own that she might call on for affection. Or protection.

'Try your ravioli before it goes cold,' she encouraged, as if she were aware of his thoughts and felt uncomfortable with them. 'Benito's father is the chef, and his spinach ravioli is to die for.'

Drakon, guessing that she was deliberately changing the subject, forked up some of the ravioli and found it to be every bit as excellent as she said it was. 'This *is* good.' He nodded his approval, not having realised how hungry he was until he bit into the succulent food.

'Would I lie to you?' Gemini grinned her satisfaction at his obvious enjoyment.

Drakon stilled, not quite sure how to answer that comment. Or if he should answer it at all. It had been his experience over the years that most women did indeed lie, and usually for the same reason.

Initially to pique his interest, and afterwards to hold that interest.

Gemini had been honest—brutally so on occasion—from the very beginning of their acquaintance. Something else that made her so different from any other woman he had ever known.

In fact, the whole evening turned out to be something of a surprise to Drakon as they ate more delicious food prepared and cooked by Benito's father. They discussed such far-ranging subjects as films they had both seen—in his own case privately, because he hated to go to noisy and overcrowded public cinemas—agreed the merits or otherwise of books they had both read, and discovered that they both had a love of opera.

'When Daddy was alive he and I would attend the

opera together once a month,' Gemini told him wistfully.

'But not your stepmother?'

'The only thing Angela liked about the opera was being able to dress up and show off the latest piece of jewellery my father had bought her,' Gemini said. 'Luckily even that wore off after the first couple of times, so my father and I were able to go alone together after that. Our monthly visit to the opera was the one thing he flatly refused to give up, even though Angela was so demanding of his attention.'

A stubbornness her father had no doubt paid a high price for, Drakon recognised with a frown, once again wondering what sort of woman Angela was that she had wanted to possess and own Miles to the exclusion of his only child. Certainly she was a woman he knew he wanted nothing more to do with than was absolutely necessary.

'What is your favourite opera?' he asked.

'Any and all of them,' Gemini answered without hesitation.

Drakon nodded. 'It's something that you either love or hate, is it not? Markos and I were lucky enough to be introduced to that love at an early age by our parents. We were both a little wild during our teenage years, and my mother was determined to instil at least some measure of refinement into us before it was too late,' he told her with a smile.

Gemini somehow couldn't imagine the controlled and haughty Drakon Lyonedes as ever being wild. She was surprised at how quickly and enjoyably the evening had passed, with Drakon proving to be an interesting as well as an entertaining dinner companion. To the extent, she now realised, that she had become so charmed by his company she had completely forgotten the reason they were having dinner together at all this evening!

'So.' She sat back with a smile as they lingered over their coffee. 'Will you be letting Max off the hook now so that he can go back to his usual duties?'

His long eyelashes lowered over suddenly guarded dark eyes. 'We won't complete on the purchase of Bartholomew House for another ten days.'

Gemini gave a sudden pained frown at the reminder that his company was buying her family home with the intention of turning it into a hotel. Something she had certainly forgotten in the last enjoyable three hours or so.

'So Max stays?' she said stiffly.

'For the time being, yes,' Drakon confirmed.

'It's time I asked Benito for the bill.' She smiled across at the owner of the restaurant. 'And please don't even suggest paying,' she added warningly as she sensed he was about to do exactly that. 'I prefer to pay my own way, thank you very much.'

Drakon was annoyed at the realisation that by introducing the subject of his purchase of Bartholomew House he had succeeded in bringing about a return of her feelings of resentment towards him.

Had that perhaps been his intention all along in order to keep her at a distance?

Pleasant and enjoyable as this evening had undoubtedly been, it had also confirmed that Gemini was unlike any other woman Drakon had ever met. To the extent he had found himself completely relaxing in her company. He had even talked of his family and his work with her—something he had never done before with any woman. Admittedly she had been just as open with him, but nevertheless he still found the experience slightly disturbing in a way he could not entirely explain.

The sooner this situation between Gemini and her stepmother was resolved, the sooner he could return to his own previously uncomplicated life!

CHAPTER TEN

'I ENJOYED this evening,' Drakon admitted once he had parked his car beside the pavement outside Gemini's shop and apartment, their journey from the restaurant having been made in complete, brooding silence.

He sensed that she had once again deliberately erected barriers between them—which was what he had intended, was it not? But having achieved his objective, he now found himself wishing for a return of that previously animated Gemini...

'Will you allow me to take you out to dinner tomorrow evening as my way of saying thank you for tonight?' he asked gruffly.

The streetlamp outside allowed him to see the frown between her brows as she turned to look at him.

'Wouldn't that rather defeat the whole object, when I took *you* out to dinner this evening as my way of saying thank you for dinner at your apartment last week?' she said slowly. 'We could go on saying thank you like this for ever!'

For ever was not something Drakon had ever considered with any woman...

Nevertheless, it was very necessary that Gemini spent tomorrow evening with him, at least. 'I thought we could have an early dinner and then perhaps we might attend the opera together?'

Pleasure instantly glowed in those beautiful sea-green eyes before the emotion was very firmly brought under her control and she gave him a chiding look. 'That isn't playing fair, Drakon!'

After their conversation earlier it had never been his intention to play fair! It was important to his plans for this weekend that Gemini spend tomorrow evening in his company. If he had to use what she considered unfair means in order to achieve that end, then so be it.

'So, what is your answer?' he prompted tensely.

'Isn't it a little late to get tickets for tomorrow—? No, of course it isn't,' Gemini answered her own question as Drakon merely raised those mocking dark brows at her; of *course* he could obtain tickets for the opera—for tomorrow or any other evening!

She knew it would be madness on her part to agree to spend another evening with Drakon—she enjoyed his company too much, found him far too dangerously attractive to be able to continue resisting the impulse she felt to simply lose herself in him.

And yet…

She hadn't attended the opera since her father had died—had wondered if she would ever be able to do so again when it would hold such painful emotional memories for her. And yet the thought of going to the opera with Drakon, of sharing that enjoyment with him when their earlier conversation had revealed how much he also loved it, was simply too much of a temptation for Gemini to be able to resist.

'I would love to go to the opera with you,' she accepted huskily.

'Good.' Drakon nodded his satisfaction with her answer. 'Is six o'clock too early for me to call and collect you so that we might enjoy an early supper together first?'

Saturdays were always Gemini's busiest day of the week, but she didn't have a wedding or a party to provide floral arrangements for tomorrow, and no doubt Jo would be happy to shut up shop just this once, while her employer went upstairs to get ready for her evening out.

'Six o'clock sounds perfect,' Gemini said, happiness bubbling up inside her at how much she was already looking forward to seeing him again tomorrow.

Only because he was taking her to the opera, she told herself firmly. It had absolutely nothing at all to do with the fact that she had enjoyed his company so much this evening she felt a slightly hollow feeling inside at the thought of parting from him.

And if she really thought she could fool herself, then she was being totally delusional!

Not only had she been completely physically aware of Drakon all evening, but she had enjoyed his company and conversation in a way she never had with any other man. He was intelligent and well read, as well as lazily charming when he wished to be, and she had found it heart-warming when he'd talked so affectionately of his family.

All of which meant Gemini was now seriously in danger of falling even deeper under his spell.

Who was she kidding? If she became any more deeply attracted to him she was likely to go up in flames at his slightest touch!

Which was reason enough not to give him the opportunity to touch her again this evening, at least.

'Six o'clock tomorrow,' she confirmed abruptly as

she pushed open the car door and quickly stepped out onto the pavement. 'No need to get out, Drakon; the cavalry has arrived!' she said dryly as she turned and saw Max's familiar black Range Rover pulling into the kerb a short distance behind Drakon's Mercedes.

'Nevertheless, I have every intention of seeing you safely to your door.' Drakon frowned his irritation at Max's sudden arrival as he got out of the car, his hand moving up to lightly cup her elbow as he nodded a brief acknowledgement to Max. 'My mother would be horrified if she were ever to hear of such a shocking lack of manners on my part after she took such care to instil gentlemanly behaviour in both Markos and I,' he teased gently when Gemini looked up at him questioningly.

She chuckled softly as they walked to the outer door leading up to her apartment. 'Your mother sounds utterly charming.'

A remark that instantly caused him to wonder what his mother would make of Gemini...

He had no doubt that Karelia would approve of Gemini's independence and determination. Of the way she had survived the loss of first her mother and then her father in but a few years. Of the way she remained calm in the face of her stepmother's relentless vindictiveness. And no doubt his mother would be amused by the way Gemini had quietly shown herself to be more than a match for his own indomitable will and arrogance.

Yes, he knew his mother would approve of and like Gemini as much as Markos did.

Drakon's mouth compressed, and his hand dropped away from Gemini's elbow at the thought of his cousin's open admiration for her. 'I will call for you at six o'clock tomorrow.' He turned sharply on his heel and left her.

Gemini watched the stiffness of Drakon's back as he returned to his car, got behind the wheel and drove off without so much as a backward glance in her direction.

Surely that couldn't be disappointment she was feeling—especially after her earlier decision not to allow him to touch her again—just because he hadn't so much as attempted to kiss her goodnight?

If it was then she was already far too deeply emotionally involved with him than she'd feared…

'I don't understand…' Gemini turned to look dazedly at Drakon the following evening as they sat in the back of the chauffeur-driven limousine he had collected her in.

The chauffeur had just driven into what looked to be a private airport, before stopping the car beside a small, sleek jet and getting out from behind the wheel to come round and open Gemini's door for her.

'I thought you said we were going to have an early supper before going to the opera?'

'We are,' Drakon said.

He'd already taken her breath away once tonight, when she'd opened the door to him and seen how devastatingly handsome he looked in an obviously expensively tailored black evening suit, with a snowy white shirt and white bow tie. Now he'd stunned her once again.

Gemini stepped slowly out onto the tarmac, too surprised to do anything other than allow him to clasp her elbow as he led her up the steps into the sleek plane. 'Where are we going?' she asked breathlessly as she took in the opulent comfort of what she now realised must be the Lyonedes jet Drakon had mentioned.

Four soft white leather armchairs were placed about a table where Drakon now saw Gemini seated before sitting down opposite her. There were another six armchairs for more casual seating, a thick black carpet on the floor, and an extensive bar towards the back of the cabin where a male steward stood pouring two glasses of champagne. A huge screen—no doubt where Drakon viewed some of the films they'd discussed over dinner the previous evening—took up most of the wall next to the cockpit.

'You may close the door now, Malcolm, and inform Drew that Miss Bartholomew and I are ready to leave.' Drakon smiled up at the steward as the other man placed the glasses of champagne on the table in front of them.

Gemini decided to take a sip of the bubbly wine before she attempted to speak; her throat was feeling unnaturally dry. 'Leave for where?' she queried, relieved when her voice came out sounding almost normal—she felt anything but.

How could she feel in the least normal when, instead of sitting in one of the small and expensive restaurants in London that catered to the opera crowd, she was on a private jet, the engines now roaring as the plane began to taxi down the runway in preparation for flying them off to goodness knew where?

'Verona,' Drakon told her with satisfaction as he relaxed back in his own comfortable chair.

Gemini gave a gasp, knowing there was only one place in Verona they could possibly attend the opera—and that was the open-air amphitheatre!

'I didn't think to ask—are you nervous about flying?' Drakon sat forward in concern as he saw the way the colour had suddenly drained from her cheeks.

He'd had no hesitation in complimenting her earlier

on how elegantly beautiful she looked this evening. She wore a simple black knee-length sheath of a dress, with a black silk shawl thrown casually about the bareness of her arms and shoulders. Her jewellery was matching teardrop emerald and diamond earrings and a slender bracelet, and the removal of the black silk shawl revealed she had on a matching necklace—an emerald the size of an English penny suspended from the clasp of a one-carat diamond nestling between the firm swell of her breasts.

None of which detracted from the fact that the colour had now bleached alarmingly from the creaminess of her cheeks…

'Gemini?' Drakon reached across the table to grasp both her trembling hands in his.

Her throat moved convulsively as she swallowed before speaking. 'I—ignore me. It's just…I've only ever attended the opera in Verona once before, and it was with my parents, as a treat for my twenty-first birthday,' she revealed huskily.

Drakon winced. He had thought Gemini would enjoy attending the opera in the Italian city—there truly was nowhere else in the world quite as magnificent as the amphitheatre in Verona for the opera. Instead he had only succeeded in bringing back memories of a happier time, when both her parents had still been alive and they had been a family.

'Would you rather I instructed Drew to turn the jet around and we returned to—?'

'Heavens, no!' Gemini exclaimed as she blinked back the tears that shimmered in her eyes. But they were tears of joy rather than unhappiness. 'For one thing, I wouldn't dream of denying Max his night off—'

'Your continued concern for my Head of Security is touching!'

'And for another, I can't imagine anything more wonderful than the opportunity to attend the opera in Verona again,' she continued emotionally. 'Thank you so much for arranging this, Drakon. I can't tell you how much I'm looking forward to this evening.' She turned to clasp and squeeze his hands reassuringly.

'You're welcome,' he murmured gruffly.

'What are we going to see?'

'*Aida*—don't tell me it's the same opera you attended with your parents,' Drakon said heavily when she drew her breath in sharply.

'Yes, it is.' Gemini gave a shaky smile, slightly stunned by the coincidence.

Her parents had arranged their trip to Italy six years ago, as a surprise for her, and the three of them had flown out to Venice and spent three days there before taking the train to Verona. Even then Gemini hadn't realised what her real twenty-first birthday treat was to be, as they had enjoyed a leisurely lunch and then strolled about Verona for the afternoon, viewing the remains of the Roman amphitheatre from the outside, enjoying the romanticism of the 'Romeo and Juliet' balcony, and then lingering at an outside café to enjoy a delicious Italian coffee before returning to their hotel to change for the evening.

It had been only as they'd left their hotel after an early supper, joining the hundreds of other people dressed in evening clothes and strolling towards the now brightly lit amphitheatre, that Gemini had realised they were going to attend *Aida* at the world-famous open-air amphitheatre.

It had been an enchanted evening—beyond spectacular—with Gemini sitting with her parents in starry-eyed wonder as the evening slowly darkened and amber lights reflected the ancient theatre in all its pageantry, a perfect and magical backdrop for the magnificent voices performing on the stage.

And tonight she was once again going to attend that magical place—with Drakon Lyonedes, of all people…

'This is perfect, Drakon,' she assured him as she smiled across at him tremulously. 'Absolutely perfect!'

Drakon was unable to make any response because he found himself held captive by the genuine happiness of Gemini's smile. Those sea-green eyes appeared as warm and glowing as the emeralds that adorned her ear-lobes, throat and wrist, her lips were full and sensual, her hair a beautiful white-gold halo about the delicacy of her face and the slenderness of her shoulders.

At that moment hers was a beauty that glowed brightly from within, and her pleasure and happiness were such that Drakon almost felt as if he could reach out and touch it. As he longed to reach out and touch *her*.

'Are you ready for me to begin serving dinner now, Mr Lyonedes?'

It was an effort for Drakon to drag his gaze away from Gemini in order to look up at the steward who stood beside the table, looking down at him enquir-ingly, his expression deliberately impersonal.

Instantly Drakon was made aware of the fact that not only had he been totally captivated by Gemini seconds ago, but they were still holding hands across the table! Which was totally out of character for a man who *never* showed public affection—even for his family.

'Are you ready to eat now, Gemini?' He smiled tightly as he extracted his hands from within her grasp and saw the confused blush that coloured her cheeks, the way she suddenly avoided his gaze.

She appeared self-conscious, and continued to avoid his gaze by smiling up at the steward. 'I would just like to visit the bathroom first, if that's okay?'

'Certainly, Miss Bartholomew.' Malcolm visibly responded to the friendly warmth of her smile. 'If you would just like to follow me I'll show you where it is.'

Drakon found he was unable to stop himself from watching the soft sway of her hips as she followed Malcolm down the cabin to the bathroom, admiring the simple elegance of her appearance. The black sheath dress was a perfect foil for that elegant diamond and emerald jewellery and the pale gold colour of her hair.

Once again he was assailed with the knowledge that Gemini Bartholomew was both a beautiful and unusual woman. Unusual in that if she was aware of that beauty—and how could she not be?—then it was not something she attempted to use to her advantage in the way most beautiful women did, as they wheedled and charmed whatever they could out of the men in their lives.

At least, that was how the women Drakon had so far met in his own life usually behaved. And there had been many. Far too many, he acknowledged ruefully. Which probably accounted for his cynicism where all women were concerned. A cynicism he would do well to remember, he warned himself, especially when in the company of this particular woman.

'That's better.' Gemini resumed her seat opposite Drakon, her hair newly brushed, the peach gloss on her lips refreshed. 'It must be all the excitement,' she added with a smile.

Drakon raised an eyebrow. 'I was not aware you found my company so stimulating.'

Gemini felt a prick of disappointment that her brief absence seemed to have brought about a return of his mocking humour. Although this timely reminder of exactly who and what he was like was a good thing, when minutes ago she had felt herself enchanted by both Drakon and the evening ahead.

'It was probably the champagne,' she excused lightly.

Those dark eyes narrowed. 'No doubt.'

'This is delicious!' Gemini enthused once Malcolm had served their first course of asparagus tips and prawns enhanced with a delicate minted sauce.

'The food is from the same restaurant that provided the meal you did not eat last week,' Drakon revealed.

'You must be one of their best customers.'

'Perhaps.'

Gemini absolutely refused to have her spirits dampened by that terse response. 'I was far too busy to find the time to eat today, so I intend to enjoy every mouthful.'

That dark gaze raked over her mercilessly, lingering on the emerald nestled against her breasts. She obviously had a taste for expensive jewellery—so perhaps she wasn't so different from every other beautiful woman he knew...

'No matter how busy you are, today or any other day, I very much doubt running a florist's shop allows you to purchase such expensive jewellery.'

Gemini stiffened at the insult she heard underlying Drakon's tone, slowly placing her knife and fork down onto the side of her plate. 'Exactly what are you implying?'

Broad muscled shoulders moved in a shrug beneath his black evening jacket. 'It was merely an observation.'

Gemini moistened her lips and took her time before answering him. 'I take it you're referring to the necklace and earrings I'm wearing this evening?'

'And the matching bracelet,' he drawled.

'Oh, we mustn't forget the matching bracelet.' Her eyes flashed the same colour as the emeralds that sparkled so brightly at her ears, neck and wrist.

Drakon raised mocking hands. 'There's no reason for you to become so defensive.'

'Isn't there?' Gemini asked. 'What's wrong, Drakon?' She leant back in her chair to study him speculatively. 'Is it that you're regretting your decision to take me to the opera in Verona, even though you know how much I'm looking forward to it? Perhaps you would rather we didn't go? That we asked the pilot to turn the plane around, after all, and returned to England?'

'Don't be ridiculous!' He looked deeply irritated, his eyes very dark, his mouth a thin, angry line. 'I was merely commenting on—'

'I know exactly what you were doing, Drakon—and it wasn't "*merely*" anything.' She gave him a direct look. 'The earrings, necklace and bracelet were my mother's. My father gave the earrings to my mother on their wedding day, the bracelet on their tenth wedding anniversary, and the necklace on their twenty-fifth.' Gemini frowned as she heard her own voice break emotionally. 'My father decided to give them all to me after she died. There would have been her emerald engagement ring too, but—' She broke off abruptly, irritated with Drakon for having succeeded in baiting her into revealing this much, and even more annoyed with herself for feeling defensive enough to speak of things that would be better left unsaid.

'But what?' Drakon prompted astutely.

Gemini avoided that piercing dark gaze as she picked up her knife and fork again. 'Could we just eat our dinner before it goes cold?'

'The first course is meant to be served cold.'

She shot him a fiery glance. 'I'm trying to change the subject here.'

'I am aware of that. But what?' he repeated insistently.

She had never before met a man who could take her through such a gamut of emotions in so short a space of time: puzzlement, excitement, pleasure, irritation, and now sheer frustration at his obvious determination that she would give him an answer to his question

She pressed her lips together stubbornly. 'Will there be anyone famous singing in the opera this evening?'

'You *will* answer my question, Gemini.'

Gemini gave a huff of incredulous laughter. 'I really can't believe that there are any women left who would still fall for that "me man, you woman" routine!'

'Oh, but there are.' His jaw set. 'Some men too.'

'Then more fool them,' she came back pertly. 'I assure you it isn't going to work on me!'

Drakon was certain that Gemini was using this conversation to hold something back from him. As certain as he was that minutes ago he had tried deliberately to insult her in an effort to put some distance between them. In retrospect, the insult had backfired on him when she had revealed that all the diamond and emerald jewellery she was wearing this evening had once belonged to her mother, and as such obviously had a sentimental value rather than a monetary one.

Yes, he had made a mistake by attempting to insult her, and it was a mistake he regretted—but that did not detract from the fact that he had every intention of knowing exactly what it was she wasn't telling him.

'Perhaps if I were to apologise for my earlier insensitivity?' he said awkwardly, not used to finding himself in a position where he needed to apologise to anybody.

'Perhaps.'

He nodded in satisfaction. 'Now you will tell me why you do not have your mother's engagement ring.'

Gemini looked across at him incredulously. '*That* was your apology?'

'Yes.'

'That's really the best you can do?'

His jaw tensed at her obvious teasing. 'For the moment I believe so, yes.'

She laughed softly. 'Gosh, it's so hard to resist when you've apologised so...*prettily.*'

'Gemini!' Drakon ground his teeth together at her obvious prevarication.

She gave a weary sigh. 'If you really must know...'

'I believe I must, yes.' A nerve pulsed in his tightly clenched jaw.

Gemini's face was once again pale. 'I accepted the earrings, necklace and bracelet after Mummy died because my father so obviously wanted me to have things that meant so much to both of them. But I could see how painful it was for him to even think of giving me Mummy's engagement and wedding rings.'

Drakon nodded. 'I can understand that.'

He knew that his own mother kept his father's wedding ring safely locked away in her jewellery box. Occasionally she took it out just to sit and hold it in her hands and think of the man she had loved and still did love—so deeply she had never even contemplated re-marrying.

Drakon's gaze sharpened as he thought of Miles Bartholomew's remarriage, and the vindictive woman who had become his second wife. 'Where are those rings now?'

Gemini smiled sadly. 'I think we both know you've already guessed exactly where my mother's rings are, Drakon.'

He could certainly take a good and accurate guess as to what had become of the rings. It was unbelievable. Unacceptable!

'Tell me anyway,' he ground out harshly.

Gemini sighed. 'The will my father left was made shortly after he and Angela were married. At a time when he still believed her to be an honourable woman, as well as a warm and loving one,' she added dully.

Drakon looked aghast. 'Your father expected that Angela would be honourable enough to give your mother's rings to you after he had died?'

'I believe he did, yes.'

'Which she has not done?'

Oh, it was much worse than that—not only had Angela not given those rings to Gemini, but she had taken great delight in wearing the emerald and diamond engagement ring herself…several times.

'Which she hasn't done,' Gemini confirmed flatly. 'Now, could we finish eating our dinner?' Although, in truth, she wasn't sure she had an appetite for it any more.

Any more than she had for the long evening in Drakon's company that now stretched ahead of her…

CHAPTER ELEVEN

A SECOND chauffeur-driven limousine was waiting for them at a private airport near Verona, but Gemini sat alone in the back of the luxurious car for several minutes after Drakon excused himself to make a brief telephone call.

'Everything okay?' she asked when he finally joined her.

'Perfect.' He turned to give her a brief, hard smile as the car moved smoothly forward.

The unpleasant memories resurrected by their earlier conversation about her parents and Angela had thankfully dissipated as they'd continued to chat casually during the delicious dinner Malcolm had served to them so efficiently during the flight, and now Gemini was once again anticipating the evening ahead, and the opera she had no doubts would be a feast for the senses.

It wouldn't dare be anything else when she had Drakon Lyonedes as her escort for the evening!

Which, when she thought about it, was pretty incredible, considering she had been feeling so angry and upset with him just over a week ago.

The reason for her initial animosity still existed, of course—especially as Drakon's company was about to take possession of Bartholomew House. But his personality was such, and this unexpected time in Verona so magical, that it was difficult if not impossible for Gemini even to think of reverting back to resenting him.

But that didn't mean she wasn't fully capable of resenting the dozens of glamorous women who looked at Drakon so covetously once they had reached the amphitheatre and joined the other patrons of the opera in the exclusive bar for a glass of champagne before the performance began.

Not that she could exactly blame any of those women. Tall, broad-shouldered, and dressed in that designer-label black evening suit and white silk shirt and bowtie, his dark hair slightly tousled from the warm and sultry breeze, Drakon was by far and away the most handsome and distinguished man present.

'Please don't let my being here stop you from being with any of your friends,' she said, after watching Drakon nod aloof acknowledgement as he was greeted by various people.

'They are mainly business acquaintances, not friends.' Drakon looked down the length of his arrogant nose at her and them. 'And I have no wish to be with any of them.'

It was a sentiment so obviously not shared by several of the more beautiful women present. 'I don't think the sexy redhead near the bar regards you as a business acquaintance!' Gemini teased, noting the other woman's sultry glance in his direction.

'I am not responsible for what other people think of me.' Drakon didn't so much as spare a glance in the redhead's direction. 'The champagne is to your liking?'

It was slightly exhilarating, Gemini realised, to know that a man whose attentions were as welcome as

Drakon's so obviously were was concerned only with *her* welfare. 'The champagne is perfect, thank you.' She smiled up at him warmly.

Drakon felt himself bathed in the warmth of that smile—a feeling he found surprisingly pleasurable after observing that several of the men present had been eyeing Gemini with acute interest since their arrival a few minutes ago. An interest she seemed totally unaware of. Or was perhaps just uninterested in? Whatever the reason—

'Gem? My God, Gem, is that really you?'

Drakon stiffened as this excited greeting interrupted his train of thought. A greeting directed at Gemini.

She confirmed that it was as she turned, her expression slightly puzzled, only to have her face light up with pleasure as she obviously recognised the blond-haired man now making his way determinedly towards her through the crowd of people.

'Good grief! What on earth are you doing here, Sam?' Gemini asked excitedly.

'The same as you. I'm here to watch the opera, of course!' The younger man seemed elusively familiar to Drakon as he reached out to grasp both of Gemini's hands in his and beamed down at her. 'My God, Gem, you can't believe how good it is to see you again—and in Verona of all places!' He laughed exuberantly.

'Unbelievable, isn't it?' Gemini acknowledged the beauty of their surroundings.

At the same time she became aware of the dark and brooding man standing stiffly disapproving beside her.

She glanced up at Drakon from beneath lowered lashes, able to feel the leashed displeasure just below the surface of his urbanity and knowing by the coldness of his expression and the chill in those glittering black eyes as he regarded the other man haughtily that he resented Sam's intrusion.

She left her hands clasped within Sam's as she made the introductions. 'Drakon—Sam Middleton. Sam, this is Drakon Lyonedes.'

'As in Lyonedes Enterprises?' Sam gave him a startled glance even as he released her to hold out a perfunctory hand in greeting.

'Middleton,' Drakon returned tersely, neither confirming nor denying his identity as he briefly returned the handshake.

'Pleased to meet you.' Sam continued to look into that harshly chiselled face for several seconds before giving a perceptible shake of his head as he turned to look back at Gemini, a dozen unasked questions in his widened bright blue eyes. 'Maybe we can get together for a longer chat during the interval?' he urged, obviously eager to pump her for answers.

'I—'

'That will not be possible, I'm afraid.' Drakon was the one to answer dismissively. 'Gemini and I will be meeting other friends then.'

She gave him a surprised look; that was the first she'd heard of it. Although, as Drakon had been the one to fly her here to Verona in his private jet, she could hardly complain if he had now decided he wanted to talk to some of his business acquaintances later on, after all.

'Sorry about that.' She gave Sam a regretful smile.

'I'll be back in London next week, so maybe we can meet up again then?' Sam suggested.

'Perhaps. *If* Gemini is back in London by next week,' Drakon said frostily at the same time as his arm moved about the slenderness of her waist.

Gemini gave him another startled glance, surprised at the possessiveness of that gesture as much as by what he had said. 'But—'

'If you will excuse us?' Drakon murmured as the bell sounded to announce the start of the performance, not even waiting for Sam's reply before moving away to join the people now making their way to their seats.

Gemini had time to turn to shoot Sam an apologetic glance over her shoulder before glaring up at Drakon. 'What on earth was all that about?' she demanded, bewildered by his behaviour.

He spared her only the briefest of glances as he concentrated on guiding her safely through the milling crowd. 'What was what about?' he said evasively.

'Well, for one thing, of course I'll be back in London next week. In fact I'll be back in London later this evening—'

'No, you won't.'

Gemini came to an abrupt halt, and then was forced to mutter a distracted apology to the couple whose way she was blocking.

'What do you mean I won't?' She frowned at him as he took a firm grasp of her arm and moved them to a less crowded and thankfully more private area.

He shrugged as he released her arm. 'The opera won't finish until very late, so naturally I have arranged for us to stay at a hotel here in Verona tonight.'

'What? Without so much as asking me if that was okay?' Gemini gasped incredulously.

He raised arrogant brows. 'I brought you to Verona without asking your permission, too.'

'Well...yes. But—' She flung up her hands in dismay. 'Not only have I not brought any other clothes or toiletries with me, but you *can't* just make decisions like that without even consulting me!'

'I believe I already have.'

Gemini's cheeks burned at what she considered his bloody-minded arrogance. 'You—'

'And the second thing?' he interrupted calmly.

'What?' she said, confused.

'You said "for one thing", so I assumed there must necessarily be a second thing?' he replied.

Gemini ground her teeth in frustration at his obvious lack of interest in discussing their overnight stay any further. 'The second thing is what was all that about with Sam just now? You deliberately gave him the impression that we're—well, that we're—'

'Involved?' he supplied dryly.

'Yes!' she hissed, uncomfortable with Drakon's continued calm when she was feeling anything but.

He looked down at her wordlessly for several long seconds. 'We had dinner together last week. And again yesterday evening. We have had dinner together again this evening. We are now in Verona, attending the opera together. And somewhere in amongst those evenings together we have twice been intimate with each other, for want of a better expression. Do all of those things not indicate that we might possibly be involved?' He arched those arrogant dark brows.

Gemini looked annoyed. They had done all those things together, yes, but as far as she was aware not one of those earlier evenings had been arranged and agreed between them. Dinner last week had been to discuss Lyonedes Enterprises buying Bartholomew House. She had organised their dinner together yesterday evening at the Italian restaurant because she had been angry with

Drakon for setting his watchdogs onto her. Which only left this evening…

Admittedly Drakon had actually invited her out this evening. And she had accepted. She just hadn't expected it would involve being whisked off to a private airport and wined and dined on the Lyonedes jet before arriving in Verona to attend the opera.

But that didn't mean she and Drakon were involved. Did it?

She shook her head firmly. 'That's still no reason for you to have behaved like—like a Neanderthal in front of Sam!'

Drakon drew in a sharp breath. 'A Neanderthal?'

Gemini's anger left her as quickly as it had flared into being when she saw his stunned disbelief at her accusation. 'A Neanderthal.' She nodded confirmation as she deliberately repeated the word. 'That "me man, you woman" thing again. Or, in this case, "you *my* woman"! Which, besides being patently untrue, was especially inappropriate seeing as Sam happens to be my cousin,' she added.

Drakon's expression of haughty disdain turned to one of puzzlement. 'I didn't realise—your surnames are not the same.'

'Could that be because Sam's mother is my mother's sister?' she asked sarcastically.

'I thought he looked vaguely familiar…' Drakon looked down at her blankly for several seconds. 'Yes, I see now that was due to the family resemblance.'

'The family that by this time tomorrow will all have been informed that I'm staying in Verona with Drakon Lyonedes! And don't you dare laugh,' Gemini warned as she saw those chiselled lips begin to twitch. 'The only family I have left are my Aunt Beatrice, Uncle Joseph and Sam—and now they're all going to think that for some reason I've allowed myself to become Drakon Lyonedes's latest bimbo!'

Drakon's humour faded as quickly as it had appeared, his eyes turning to ebony chips of ice as he looked down at her. 'As far as I am aware I have never associated with bimbos,' he informed her frostily.

'Kept woman. Mistress. Whatever,' Gemini said crossly. 'I don't enjoy having the only family I have left in the world believing I'm no better than Angela!'

Drakon looked down at her searchingly, noting the over-bright sheen to those glorious sea-green eyes, the slight pallor to her cheeks, and realized—no matter how much he might resent her accusations—that her distress concerning what her small immediate family might think of her was very real.

He drew in a deep breath. 'We will seek out your cousin at the interval and I will endeavour to put the record straight with regard to our relationship.'

She raised surprised brows. 'And exactly how do you intend doing that?'

'By informing him that our association is primarily a business one. Also that we have separate rooms booked at the hotel tonight. No...?' he said with a frown as Gemini gave a firm shake of her head.

'No,' she said. 'I'm afraid that all sounds a little like protesting too much.'

'I could always apologise for my earlier manner—explain that I had no idea he was your cousin—'

'Which would only give the impression that we *are* involved, after all!' She sighed. 'Never mind, Drakon. I'll sort it out with Sam when he gets back to London next week.' She ran an agitated hand through her hair. 'Let's just go and listen to the opera, hmm?'

The last thing Drakon had intended this evening was to create a reason for any more unpleasantness in Gemini's life—in truth, bringing her to Verona, well away from England, had been deliberately designed to do the very opposite. But that unexpected meeting with her cousin certainly seemed to have cast a shadow over her enjoyment.

Because, as she had so succinctly pointed out, Drakon had behaved like a Neanderthal when confronted with a younger man who seemed to be on far too intimate an acquaintance with her!

He had assumed, from the warmth of their greeting to each other, that Gemini and Sam must have been romantically involved in the past. And he had not liked it. Not one little bit. Which was really no excuse for his proprietorial behaviour towards her.

'You're right. We should take our seats now,' he said.

Drakon's inner feelings of disquiet resulted in him spending the first hour of the opera looking at Gemini more than he did the spectacle taking place on the stage: the smooth sheen of her white-gold hair, the creaminess of her brow and cheek, the clear brightness of those seagreen eyes as she gazed at the performers with rapt attention, the sensual fullness of her lips, the slender arch of her throat, and the tempting swell of her breasts.

The knowledge of her innocence told Drakon she was a young woman of principle. Her love and respect for her father, despite his disastrous second marriage, indicated that she was a woman of loyalty. She was a young woman who, because she had grown up protected and cosseted by her father's wealth, could so easily have chosen to become one of the idle and bored debutantes Drakon had met so many times in the past at social events all over the world. But she had instead chosen to forge her own life and career by opening her own shop and working—working hard—with the flowers she so obviously loved.

All of which made her the most beautiful and unaffected young woman Drakon had ever met.

And he wanted her badly.

He ached to hold her softness in his arms as he moulded her body against his. To kiss every inch of her face and throat before claiming her lips with his. To cup her bared breasts in his hands as he slowly pleasured their stiff peaks. To caress the slenderness of her waist and hips before gently stroking the heat between her thighs—

'Isn't this wonderful!' Gemini breathed, having placed her hand excitedly on Drakon's arm as she turned to look at him with eyes that seemed to glow the same intense green as her emeralds. The earlier tension between them, and the reason for it, had obviously been forgotten. And forgiven, he sincerely hoped.

'Wonderful,' he echoed gruffly as his hand moved to capture and keep the warmth of her fingers pressed against his arm, but he was looking at Gemini and not at the stage above.

She gave him another one of her warm smiles before turning back eagerly to the opera, seemingly unaware that her hand still lay clasped within Drakon's.

Exactly when, he wondered, had this woman slipped beneath his guard of cynicism? When, exactly, had he ceased to regard Gemini as nothing but an intrusive nuisance, one he wished out of his life as quickly as she had thrust herself into it? When had that protectiveness he had felt after learning of Angela Bartholomew's viciousness towards her become so all-consuming?

He had no need to wonder *why* it had happened.

He had realised only too well during this past hour of watching her, of looking at her, exactly the reasons she was now such an important part of his life.

If not the *most* important…

'Wasn't that absolutely amazing?' Gemini exclaimed several hours later as she and Drakon emerged onto the lamplit cobbled street outside the amphitheatre, her hand resting on the crook of his arm so that they wouldn't be separated amongst the crowds of happy people milling around them.

Drakon had seemed distant towards her during the interval, although true to his word they had sought out Sam. Drakon had insisted on the younger man joining them for a glass of champagne. As she had requested, Drakon had offered no apology for his earlier behaviour, but instead had warmly encouraged her cousin to talk of the places he had already visited during what was apparently a touring holiday of Italy—something the enthusiastic Sam had been only too happy to do.

Gemini shot Drakon a concerned glance now. 'You know, I was only being half serious earlier when I called you a Neanderthal.'

To her relief he gave her a wry smile. 'It was a perfectly justified accusation on your part.' He grimaced. 'I behaved badly.'

'You made up for it by being charming to Sam during the interval,' she said.

Drakon came to a halt as he looked down at her quizzically. 'Are you always so ready to forgive?'

She shrugged. 'Life's really too short to do anything else, don't you think?'

His mouth thinned. 'Some people are beyond forgiveness.'

'Well…yes.' Gemini didn't need to ask which person he was referring to! 'But in those circumstances surely the best thing to do is simply cut them out of your life rather than reduce yourself to their level?'

Drakon looked down at her in open admiration. 'Enjoyable as the opera undoubtedly was, *you* are what I have found amazing this evening, Gemini.'

She gave him a startled look. 'I am?'

'Oh, yes.'

'Despite the Neanderthal remark?' she teased.

He laughed softly. 'In spite of it.'

'Oh…'

Drakon tilted his head as he looked down at her quizzically for several long seconds. 'You really have no idea how unusual a woman you are, do you?' he finally said warmly.

Gemini wasn't quite sure what to make of Drakon in his current mood. His cynicism she had learnt to cope with. His arrogance, too. Even his mockery was easily deflected if she didn't allow it to get to her. What Gemini had no idea how to deal with was this admiring, almost gentle Drakon…

'I'm just me, Drakon,' she protested.

'Exactly.'

Gemini frowned up at him in the lamplight, her heart starting to beat loudly in her chest. She saw the warmth in his obsidian eyes as he gazed steadily back at her, a nerve pulsing in his jaw, those chiselled lips softened and slightly parted.

Oh, good Lord!

Physically innocent she might be, but she would have to be a moron not to recognise the look in his eyes for the desire that it was. Ditto the parted invitation of his lips. It was a desire the nerve pulsing in his jaw would seem to indicate he was holding firmly under his control. Unless Gemini were to indicate she wished it otherwise.

The question was, did she want to do that?

When she had come to Verona six years ago it had been as a beloved daughter being given a special birthday treat by her parents. Being here now with Drakon was absolutely nothing like that.

Their slight disagreement apart, she had been absolutely, totally aware of him all evening—despite the magical opera. That awareness had been humming beneath the surface of her skin all evening, with a tingling that made her sensitive nipples ache and heat pool between her thighs. It was an ache that she knew Drakon was more than capable of satisfying.

She looked up at him in the golden glow of the lamplight. The strong angles of his face were thrown into shadows, his dark eyes were looking down at her, and she knew that she wanted him to make love with her more than she had ever wanted anything in her life before.

She moistened her lips before speaking, her cheeks feeling warm as she saw the hungry way his gaze followed the tip of her tongue as it swept over that pouting softness. 'So you booked separate rooms for us at the hotel, did you?' she asked.

It was only as Drakon breathed in deeply that he realised he had not been breathing at all for the last minute or so. 'I requested a suite with two bedrooms.'

Gemini chuckled. 'Hedging your bets, Drakon?'

Had he been? Had he hoped that the evening would be so successful, so enjoyable, that he and Gemini would spend the night together?

Certainly not consciously. 'I doubt that there will be

a four-poster bed in either of them,' he told her apologetically.

'Probably not, no,' she agreed quietly.

'Or rose petals to perfume the room,' he added gruffly.

'I'm sure I won't notice with the light off,' Gemini murmured.

The fact that Drakon had bothered to remember her romantic fantasies was enough for now. More than enough to sustain her tingling awareness as they walked the short distance to an exclusive hotel.

That awareness had been elevated to an almost overwhelming swell of anticipation by the time they had booked in and Drakon had used a keycard to allow them to enter the sitting room of a suite on the top floor.

'No.' Gemini moved to stop his hand as he would have reached out and turned on the light. The moonlight streaming into the room through the two floor-to-ceiling windows provided the necessary illumination as she stepped into his arms. 'Make love to me, Drakon,' she whispered, her face lifting invitingly to his as her arms moved about his waist.

Drakon's hands moved up to cradle each side of her face as he gazed down at her hungrily. The softness of her creamy cheeks felt like velvet against his palms as he committed the perfection of her face to memory, to be taken out at some later date to please or torment him.

'You are so overwhelmingly beautiful, Gemini, inside as well as out,' he muttered, and the rasp of their breath was the only sound in the room as his head lowered and his lips at last laid claim to hers.

Their passion, their need for each other, was like a dam bursting, and the kiss that had started so gently quickly became something else as they took eagerly,

hungrily, from each other, and gave back just as much
in return. Lips devoured, teeth gently bit, and tongues
duelled in devouring demand.

Drakon groaned as he felt himself spiralling quickly
out of control. Gemini's fingers became entangled in
the hair at his nape as they continued to kiss hungrily.
His skin felt hot and feverish, his shaft a hard and pulsing ache as he pressed into the heated softness between
her thighs, wanting—oh, God, how he wanted her. It
was suddenly all too much...

'Drakon?' Gemini's eyes were huge bewildered pools
of dark green as he suddenly wrenched his mouth away
from hers and put her firmly away from him.

He breathed in raggedly before looking down at her
from between lowered lids. 'As I pointed out earlier, we
do not have the four-poster bed or the perfume of rose
petals that you said were required for your seduction,'
he reminded her distantly.

'My seduction?' she repeated painfully.

Drakon's mouth compressed but he didn't reply.

She clasped shaking hands in an attempt to steady
them. 'I don't understand...' Minutes ago, seconds
ago, he had seemed on the point of devouring her—
and goodness knew she had been more than willing.
The passion between them had been so intense they had
seemed in danger of going up in flames.

He dropped his gaze. 'For us to go to bed together
now would be wrong on levels I cannot begin to explain.'

'For whom?' Gemini prompted shrewdly. 'Is it that
you don't want the so-called responsibility of taking
my innocence? That you maybe even think, in my na-
ivety, I might imagine myself to be in love with you?'
she pressed.

Drakon stood unmoving as her words rained down like daggers entering his flesh. 'It is a possibility, is it not?'

'No!' she gave a shocked gasp. 'No, Drakon, it isn't a possibility!' She stepped back, her gaze anguished as the heat of tears drenched those sea-green depths. 'You—' She broke off as the sound of his mobile phone intruded into the tension. 'You should answer that. It might be one of the women from the opera earlier, wanting to meet up with you. An *experienced* woman!' she spat.

'Possibly,' he said coolly.

Gemini gave him one last fulminating glare before turning on her heel and hurrying across the room to enter one of the two bedrooms and slam the door behind her.

Leaving Drakon alone in the moonlight as each and every one of those daggers pierced deeply into a part of him he had believed until tonight to be invincible...

CHAPTER TWELVE

GEMINI felt emotionally exhausted by the time the chauffeur-driven limousine drew to a halt beside the pavement outside her shop at twelve o'clock the following day. She hadn't slept at all the previous night, listening as Drakon talked briefly on the telephone before she heard the sound of the other bedroom door softly closing—evidence that he obviously wasn't taking her up on her suggestion that he go out again.

Neither of them had had any appetite for the breakfast Drakon had ordered to be delivered to their suite at eight o'clock this morning, and the drive to the airport and their flight back to England had been made in tense silence.

She could have sat down and cried for the awful way their evening together in Verona had ended. Apart from that brief awkwardness with Sam it had been such a magical time: the delicious dinner on the plane, the beautiful sights and smells of Verona, the pageantry of the opera, the romantic walk along the cobbled streets to their hotel with the warmth of Drakon's arm draped possessively about her waist, the wild heat of passion once they were finally alone together in their suite.

And then the icy coldness of Drakon's rejection.

Even now, after hours of thinking of virtually noth-

ing else, Gemini didn't understand it, let alone accept
it. He had known from the outset that she'd had no other
lovers, and it certainly hadn't seemed to bother him during the walk back to the hotel, or when they had kissed
so passionately.

She turned to look at him now as he sat so distant
and unmoving beside her in the back of the limousine.
'Drakon—'

'We should go up to your apartment now,' he cut in
as the chauffeur got out of the car and opened Gemini's
door for her.

'We?' Gemini had assumed from his aloofness the
past twelve hours that once they were back in England
Drakon would be anxious to get rid of the responsibility of her before returning to New York.

'Max has arrived.' He nodded to where the black
Range Rover had just parked in front of the limousine.
His grim-faced Head of Security was getting out from
behind the wheel. 'The two of us need to talk to you
privately,' Drakon added before opening the door beside him and striding over to greet the older man.

Gemini got slowly out of the car, vaguely smiling
her thanks at the chauffeur at the same time trying, and
failing, to hear what Drakon and Max were saying to
each other. Their voices too soft for her to make out any
of their conversation, although their expressions didn't
look reassuring.

She frowned as the men walked briskly back to join
her. 'Drakon, what—?'

'We will go inside, where we cannot be overheard.'
He took a firm grasp of her arm.

Considering it was lunchtime on a Sunday—a time
when most people were either at home or in the local
pub eating lunch—the area was virtually deserted, with

only two uninterested joggers passing by on the other side of the road—which was probably as well, when Gemini and Drakon were both so obviously wearing the clothes they had worn the evening before.

'Aren't you being a bit cloak-and-dagger?' she protested.

'Privacy would be best.' Max was the one to answer her gruffly.

'I don't think so.' Gemini stubbornly dug her heels in as she glared at first one man and then the other. 'In fact I'm not going anywhere until one of you tells me what's going on.'

A grudging amusement entered Max's steely blue eyes before he turned to raise questioning brows at his employer.

Drakon's jaw clenched. 'You are the most stubborn woman!' He sighed impatiently. 'Bartholomew House was broken into last night,' he revealed economically.

Gemini recoiled slightly in shock. 'I—is Angela all right?' she gasped breathlessly.

Drakon's impatience turned to incredulity at her concern for a woman who had been nothing but vicious and cruel towards her. A woman who had tried to do everything in her power, since Miles's death, to make Gemini miserable in every way possible. A woman, in fact, who deserved no one's sympathy—least of all Gemini's.

'Your stepmother was not at home at the time,' Drakon assured her coolly.

'Thank goodness!' She looked relieved. 'Was anything taken?'

'That is what we need to talk to you about,' he answered pointedly.

Gemini continued to look at him dazedly for several long seconds, a frown between her eyes. 'I don't understand...' She shook her head. 'How do you even know about the break-in if it only happened last night?' she finally said slowly. 'Let alone that Angela wasn't at home at the time?'

He raised dark brows. 'That is the reason that Max and I would prefer this conversation took place in private.'

Sea-green eyes widened as Gemini obviously took in the full import of what he had said. She glanced at the stoic Max and then back at Drakon. 'Perhaps it might be better if we did go up to my apartment, after all.'

'A canny lass; I knew there was a reason I liked you!' Max nodded approval.

'That's a pity—because I'm still reserving judgement on *you*!' Gemini threw back as she unlocked the door leading up to her apartment.

Max gave a throaty chuckle—the first that Drakon could remember hearing from him in the five years Max had worked for him. 'Give it time, lass, maybe I'll grow on you.'

'I wouldn't count on it,' Gemini muttered as she led the way upstairs, still feeling slightly stunned about the break-in at Bartholomew House and the unspoken implications of Drakon's knowledge of it. Let alone what Max's presence here might indicate.

'Okay!' She threw her wrap and bag down on the coffee table in her sitting room before turning to face the two men. 'One of you tell me exactly what's going on. And I sincerely hope your explanation doesn't include telling me that Max, for reasons as yet unknown, was the one who broke into Bartholomew House last night! Drakon?' she prompted.

Max was now avoiding her gaze as he took a thick envelope from the breast pocket of his leather jacket and handed it to Drakon, before turning his back on the room to stare out of the window onto the street down below.

Drakon smiled ruefully as he recognised the light of challenge in Gemini's eyes. 'I have no intention of telling you that Max was anywhere near Bartholomew House last night.'

She eyed him reprovingly. 'The wording of that statement isn't exactly reassuring.'

'It wasn't intended to be,' Drakon said dryly. 'I believe you should look at this before you say anything else,' he continued firmly as Gemini would have spoken, and reached into the envelope. He took out what looked to be a legal document of some kind before holding it out to her.

Gemini made no effort to take the document but eyed it as if it were a snake about to uncoil and sink its fangs into her. Her mouth had gone dry. 'Tell me what it is first...'

Drakon drew in a sharp breath before answering her. 'It was locked away in the safe at Bartholomew House, and it is the last will and testament of Miles Gifford Bartholomew, signed and witnessed by two members of his household staff two weeks before his death. In it he bequeaths an apartment in Paris and a villa in Spain, plus a yearly sum for the rest of her life, to his wife, Angela Gail Bartholomew, and Bartholomew House, plus the remainder of his estate, to his only daughter— namely Gemini Bartholomew.'

All the colour bleached from her cheeks, and a loud buzzing noise sounded in her head. The room began to dip and sway, before—thankfully—complete darkness descended.

* * *

Gemini didn't believe she had ever fainted in her life before, but as she roused herself groggily, and found herself lying on the sofa in her sitting room, Drakon crouched beside her, a concerned expression on his face, she knew that was exactly what had happened.

Because Drakon had told her of the existence of a more recent will than the one which had previously been presented by her father's lawyers...

Gemini blinked up at him. 'Is it really true? There was a newer will all the time?' She pushed the hair back from her face as he helped her to sit up.

'There was a newer will,' Drakon confirmed as he straightened, his hands clasped tightly behind his back in an effort to contain the rage he felt towards Angela Bartholomew. A rage which had been steadily growing since learning the truth from Max during the other man's telephone call to him late the previous evening. 'A legal will which, for obvious reasons, your stepmother decided it was in her best interests to repress,' he added harshly.

Gemini looked up at him with tear-wet eyes. 'Daddy kept his promise after all...'

Drakon's hands tightened painfully. 'Yes, he did.'

Those tears overflowed to fall softly down the paleness of her cheeks. 'Bartholomew House is really mine?'

'Yes.'

'That's— I can't tell you how— Oh!' She raised startled sea-green eyes. 'But that must also mean, if Angela is no longer the legal owner of Bartholomew House, that the contract Lyonedes Enterprises has with her to buy the house and land is no longer valid?'

Drakon's smile was humourless. 'No, it is not.'

Gemini caught her bottom lip between her teeth. 'I'm so sorry, Drakon.'

'You're *sorry*?' he exploded incredulously. 'That woman attempted to deny you your true heritage, that which is legally and morally yours, taking great delight in doing so, and you are *apologising* to me? Unbelievable!'

'Not just a canny lass but a generous-hearted one too,' Max murmured admiringly from where he still stood beside the window.

'A woman like no other,' Drakon acknowledged huskily as he turned to look at the other man. A wealth of understanding passed between them in that single brief glance. 'This is a time for rejoicing in your good fortune, Gemini.' Drakon turned back to her. 'Not a time for you to concern yourself with any legal ramifications for Lyonedes Enterprises.'

A frown appeared on the creaminess of her brow. 'But how could you possibly have known where the will was?'

'You can thank Max for that,' Drakon said. 'I merely voiced my suspicions. He was the one who made discreet enquiries of some of your father's present and ex-employees.'

'I struck gold with a young woman—Jackie—who was your father's personal assistant and stayed on for several months to assist your stepmother after he died,' Max said dourly. 'She doesn't work for Mrs Bartholomew any longer, but once I explained who I was, and the reason for my interest in the possibility of a newer will, she was only too happy to supply the combination number to the safe in your father's study. I gather she has her own reasons for disliking your stepmother.'

Gemini grimaced. 'I believe Angela's way of thanking Jackie for her assistance was to have an affair with her fiancé only weeks after my father died.'

'That would do it,' Max agreed.

'But is this will still legal if it was…obtained in the way it was?' she asked.

'It is most certainly legal.' Drakon nodded firmly. 'And I don't think Angela Bartholomew would care to go to the authorities with accusations of theft when to do so would mean she would have to explain why she did not admit to knowing of the existence of this will months ago.'

'I wonder why she didn't simply burn it?' Gemini mused.

'I don't know, and I don't particularly care,' he rasped. 'Admittedly it would have been better for all concerned if your father had gone to his lawyers and left the signed will with them, but perhaps he believed a private will, with the signature of two members of his household as witnesses, would be a safer way of dealing with the matter.'

'Less obvious to the eagle-eyed Angela, you mean?' Gemini guessed. 'Yes, I'm sure you're right. Although she obviously found the new will anyway, after Daddy died so suddenly.'

'Unfortunately, yes,' he agreed. 'Max has also ascertained this morning that she dismissed the two witnesses to the will from their employment at Bartholomew House shortly after your father's death. In an effort, no doubt, to prevent them from stepping forward with knowledge of the existence of a new will.'

'Knowing Daddy, they wouldn't have been aware of the exact contents of the will anyway,' she said. 'It was really in the safe at Bartholomew House all this time, then?'

'Yes.'

She glanced across at the stony-faced Max where he still stood in front of the window. 'And you were the one who...*found* it there?'

He grimaced. 'I think I'll take the fifth on that one, if you don't mind.'

Gemini knew that was the only admission she was likely to get that he had indeed been the one to enter Bartholomew House the previous evening.

She stood up to cross the room and throw her arms around his waist. 'Thank you, Max!' She hugged him tight. 'Thank you so much!'

He stood uncomfortably in her arms for several seconds. 'I think your hug is misdirected, lass,' he finally murmured gruffly, and patted her back awkwardly.

Gemini knew exactly who she had to thank for her sudden change of fortune—knew perfectly well that Max had been acting directly under Drakon's orders.

She gave Max another brief hug before turning to face Drakon, knowing that what he had done, what he had asked Max to do, was going to cause him and Lyonedes Enterprises serious problems.

The new will proved Angela a liar and a cheat. And because of that Lyonedes Enterprises would no longer acquire the much-coveted site in London on which it had intended building a hotel complex. Drakon himself could come in for serious legal ramifications if Angela decided to go to the authorities after all. In fact, the only one to benefit from the actions of the past twelve hours would appear to be Gemini herself...

'I don't know how to thank you—'

'No thanks are necessary,' he assured her stiffly.

She threw Max an amused glance. 'Now you know why I thanked you first,' she murmured exasperatedly.

'Don't bring me into this.' The older man held up his hands in mock protest before turning back towards the window. 'Uh-oh—I believe trouble has arrived,' he announced.

'Angela?' Gemini said knowingly.

'Oh, yes,' Max confirmed as he turned back to look at Drakon. 'Do you want me to go down and—'

'Let her come up.' Gemini was the one to answer him. 'Drakon, if Angela has somehow worked out who was responsible for the break-in at Bartholomew House last night then we'd only be delaying this confrontation by ignoring her now,' she reasoned, just as he was about to issue instructions to Max.

Drakon's admiration for Gemini grew by the minute, it seemed. Admittedly she had fainted once she knew of her father's more recent will, and realised she was the owner of Bartholomew House after all, but that had been understandable. Her stoicism since then had been indomitable.

As he had told Max earlier, Gemini truly was a woman like no other…

The intercom buzzed in announcement of Angela's presence downstairs.

Drakon sighed. 'Gemini is right, Max. We might as well get this over with now.'

'I think that's best.' Gemini walked over to the speaker on the intercom. 'Come up, Angela,' she instructed the other woman coldly, and pressed the button to open the external door.

Drakon frowned. 'Gemini—'

'Don't worry, Drakon,' she said as her stepmother

could be heard coming up the stairs. 'Now that I know the truth I'm more than capable of handling her.'

Drakon was sure that she was; he only feared what further emotional damage Angela might do to her in the meantime...

The older woman's expression was contemptuous as she entered the room. 'I should have known that *you* would be here too.' She gave Drakon a scathing glance. 'And no doubt this is one of your henchman!' she said, glaring at Max.

'Mrs Bartholomew.' Max gave a terse nod, his steely gaze narrowed in warning.

Blue eyes glittered angrily as Angela turned to Gemini. 'You do realise that I could have you arrested for theft, as well as for breaking and entering at Bartholomew House?'

'There has been a break-in at Bartholomew House?' Drakon was the one to address her smoothly.

'You know damn well there has!'

He raised dark brows. 'And why on earth should I know that?'

'Oh, please!' Angela snapped. 'You even arranged for your cousin to take me to dinner last night in order to make sure I was out of the house.'

Drakon turned as he sensed Gemini looking at him incredulously, nodding slightly in confirmation when she mouthed, *Markos took her out to dinner?*

'What does your date with Markos last night have to do with me?' he asked.

'It worked very effectively as a means of ensuring you could sneak in and do your little Houdini act with certain contents of my safe!'

Drakon shrugged. 'I assure you I have absolutely no

control over my cousin's actions. Nor do I understand
what you mean by my "Houdini act".'

Angela gave a disbelieving snort. 'I didn't even dis-
cover there was anything missing until I went to the
safe this morning to return the jewellery I wore to go
out last night.'

'And you believe *I* am the one responsible for those
items being missing?' He raised haughty brows.

'I know you are!'

'I am afraid you are under a misapprehension, Mrs
Bartholomew,' Drakon bit out coldly. 'Neither I, nor indeed Gemini, were even in England last night. We flew
to Verona for the evening. For the opera, you know. We
returned only a short time ago.'

Gemini looked at Drakon sharply as it became glar-
ingly obvious to her exactly why they had flown to
Verona and stayed the night there; by doing so Drakon
had ensured that they both had an alibi for the break-in.

Angela seemed to notice their evening clothes for
the first time, and her cheeks became flushed. 'Then
you had your henchman do it for you—'

'I believe this conversation is over, Mrs
Bartholomew,' Drakon cut in repressively.

'A word of advice, Drakon,' Angela jeered. 'Never
try to deceive a deceiver.'

'At last we seem to be agreed on something,' he replied.

Angela's face darkened angrily. 'Why, you—'

'That's quite enough!' Gemini stepped forward to
grip Angela's arm as she swung it with the obvious intention of slapping Drakon's face. 'You may have done
your best to make me miserable, Angela, but you will
never—*ever*—attack any of my friends.' She thrust

her face in front of the shorter woman's. 'Is that understood?'

'Is that what you call him? 'Your "friend"?' Angela sneered.

Gemini drew in a sharp breath at the deliberate insult, but at the same time she knew the accusation was far from the truth; Drakon wasn't, never had been, and now probably never would be her lover, as Angela was implying he was. Unfortunately...

"Not having any of your own, you probably wouldn't recognise friendship if it bit you on the nose,' she said coldly. 'But, yes, Drakon is my friend. And this is my home. As such, you will not insult one of my friends in my home. Is that understood? *Is it?*' she pressed.

A grudging respect entered the glittering blue eyes that stared up into Gemini's. 'Yes,' Angela finally grated tightly.

'Good.' Gemini released her arm and stepped back. 'Now, for my father's sake, not yours, I'm willing to let you walk out of here and take up permanent residence in either the Paris apartment or the Spanish villa you apparently own. If,' she continued firmly as Angela would have spoken, 'you don't do either of those things, then you will leave me with no choice but to go to the police and tell them of your duplicity.'

'If you did that you would only implicate yourself and your "friends" in the robbery at my home.'

'Actually, that would be *my* home,' Gemini corrected. 'And, as such, the contents of the safe there would also be *my* property,' she added challengingly.

Angela's face paled. 'But you didn't know any of that when the will was taken.'

'I know it now,' Gemini pointed out. 'Which I believe will be all that matters in the eyes of the law,' she added, with much more confidence that she actually felt. 'But feel free to challenge my claim if that's what you want to do.'

Angela scowled. 'Exactly when did you develop claws?'

'Oh, they were always there,' Gemini assured the other woman. 'Merely sheathed for my father's sake. So which is it to be, Angela? Paris or the villa in Spain? Whichever one you choose, I will give you two days to vacate Bartholomew House and leave England for good,' she added. 'Oh, and I also expect you to return the rather large deposit you received from Lyonedes Enterprises when you agreed to sell them a property you knew you didn't actually own.'

The older woman seemed to fight an inner battle with herself for several long seconds, as if she were exploring each avenue of escape open to her, and her shoulders finally dropped in defeat as she obviously found they all ended in a cul-de-sac.

'You should have just burnt the new will,' Gemini said.

'Yes, I should.' Angela sighed. 'I just couldn't quite bring myself to do it. For what it's worth, I *did* love Miles,' she finally admitted tightly. 'In my own way.'

Gemini gave a weary shake of her head. 'I'm not sure whether that makes your behaviour better or worse.'

'No,' Angela acknowledged heavily before glancing at Drakon and Max. 'Touché, gentlemen. Now, if you will all excuse me,' she drawled, 'it appears I have a lot of packing to do. And a visit to make to my bank to return funds to Lyonedes Enterprises. I take it you will deal with the legal side of things?' She looked enquiringly at Drakon.

'Already being dealt with,' he confirmed.

Angela nodded again before turning on one three-inch heel and leaving. The door downstairs closed quietly behind her seconds later.

Gemini sank down weakly into one of her armchairs, more relieved than she could say that the situation had finally been resolved in such a way that it took Angela out of her life for good and at the same time gave her back Bartholomew House.

And it was all thanks to Drakon…

CHAPTER THIRTEEN

DRAKON had watched and listened proudly as Gemini completely dominated the woman who had taken advantage of the deep love Gemini felt for her father in order to manipulate and steal from her.

But at the same time he'd felt a heavy weight in his chest at Gemini's insistence that she considered him only as a friend.

'I'll go too now, if that's okay?' Max murmured.

'Gemini?' Drakon prompted gruffly.

She roused herself enough to look up and smile at Max. 'Thank you once again. For everything.'

'No problem.' He nodded to them both before leaving.

Drakon was unsure what to say in order to breach the tense silence left behind by the other man's departure. Uncertainty, in any given situation, was not an emotion that sat well on his shoulders.

Gemini looked across at him. 'Do you think we'll—I'll—ever hear from Angela again?'

He smiled confidently. 'Somehow I think not. You were like a tigress just now in defence of your...friends.'

She nodded. 'And I meant every word. You and Max, and poor Markos, have all been wonderful.'

'I believe I may speak for the others when I say it

was our pleasure,' Drakon said. 'I should leave now as well,' he added. 'You will no doubt need time and space in which to properly absorb your change of circumstances.'

Gemini gave herself a mental shake, knowing that this was Drakon's way of saying goodbye. 'Did Markos really take Angela out to dinner last night in order to make sure she was out of the house for several hours?'

'Yes.' Drakon's mouth twisted. 'He felt it was the least he could do after his error earlier this week.' He shrugged those broad shoulders. 'I believe he also likes you.'

And Gemini liked Markos too.

But she *loved* Drakon…

Completely.

It was a discovery, an admission she had made to herself, as she'd lain awake and alone in her bed in the hotel in Verona the previous night…

She loved everything about Drakon. The way he looked obviously made her feel weak at the knees, and when he kissed her, made love to her, she simply melted. But it was so much more than that. She loved his obvious love and loyalty towards his family, his integrity in business, his self-confidence in any situation, his ability to make Gemini feel protected while at the same time respecting her freedom of choice.

Alone in her bed last night she had realised that Drakon was everything, and more, she could ever have wished for in the man she loved.

That love had only deepened today in the knowledge that he had believed in her, cared enough—even if it was only as a friend—to ensure that Bartholomew House was returned to her.

She moistened her lips before speaking. 'Will you be returning to New York now?'

Drakon was silent for several seconds. Several long seconds. 'That depends on you,' he finally answered.

Gemini gave him a startled glance. 'Me?'

'Yes,' he confirmed wryly. 'Shall I go back to New York today, Gemini, or shall I remain here in London, so that we might perhaps start again?' His expression was strained.

'Start what again?' Gemini was aware that she sounded idiotic, virtually repeating every word Drakon said, but she was afraid of misunderstanding him, and by doing so causing embarrassment to them both.

Drakon breathed heavily. 'Everything,' he bit out forcefully. 'We met in unusual circumstances, and our relationship has continued in that unusual way ever since.' He moved forward until he was close enough to crouch down beside the chair in which she sat. 'I am asking, Gemini, if we could not begin again?' He reached out to take one of her hands in his, and became aware of the envelope he still held. 'I totally forgot…' He frowned down at the bulky envelope. 'I should have given you this earlier.'

'Haven't you given me enough already?' Gemini looked totally bewildered.

Drakon reached into the envelope and drew out a small green box before resting it in his palm and holding it out to her. 'I believe this also belongs to you,' he said.

Gemini could only stare down blankly at the ring box in Drakon's hand, still befuddled by the possibilities of what Drakon had just said to her. It had seemed as if he wanted another chance with her.

'What is it?' she prompted breathlessly.

He smiled gently. 'I am sure that you already know.'

Yes, she did know. Was positive that inside the ring box would be her mother's emerald and diamond engagement ring and her plain gold wedding band!

She blinked in an effort to clear the tears that suddenly stung her eyes. 'Was this the private telephone call you made yesterday evening when we arrived in Verona?'

'Yes,' he acknowledged simply.

Gemini reached out and took the box tentatively before slowly raising the lid. The familiarity of the rings inside caused her to close her eyes, sending those scalding tears cascading down her cheeks.

'Oh, Drakon…' She began to sob in earnest.

'Don't cry, Gemini!' He reached out and gathered her into his arms, pressed her face into the warmth of his chest. 'I thought only to make you happy,' he murmured huskily as he crushed her to him. 'Please don't cry, *agapi mou*,' he entreated. 'I cannot bear it!'

Gemini couldn't seem to stop crying. She couldn't remember anyone—not even her father, whom she had adored and who had adored her—doing anything so absolutely, unselfishly wonderful for her. Put that together with Drakon's earlier conversation, and his endearment just now, and her earlier hopes began to take flight…

She raised her head and looked at Drakon, seeing his concern for her in those dark, dark eyes. And something else…

She moistened her lips before speaking, and saw emotion darken those now jet-black eyes. 'Drakon, why, when it must have been obvious how willing I was, did you change your mind about making love to me last night?'

His expression became strained. 'In the circumstances, it would have been wrong of me to take advantage of you...'

'And?' Gemini pressed, her heart pounding loudly in her chest.

He gave a tight smile. 'I told you—there was no four-poster bed and no rose petals.'

'But I told you those things didn't matter to me any more...'

His mouth firmed. 'They matter to *me*!' he told her fiercely. 'Damn it, I love you, Gemini—and, difficult as it was to walk away from you last night, I could not in all conscience make love to you until everything else in your life had been settled.'

'You *love* me?' she repeated breathlessly, her heart seeming to falter and then stop, before starting up again, stronger, quicker.

Drakon gave a pained wince. 'I had not meant to say that to you just yet.'

She looked at him quizzically. 'Why not?'

'Because you deserve more. You deserve to be wooed and courted, to be spoilt and cosseted, before I so much as broach the subject of the depth of my feelings for you.'

The beating of Gemini's heart soared out of control. 'And what of the depth of my feelings for you?'

He blinked. 'You have feelings for me? Of course you do.' A muscle twitched in his jaw. 'They are feelings of friendship. And gratitude.'

The tears once again began to fall down her cheeks. 'Yes, of course I'm grateful to you—how could I not be when you've done something so wonderfully unselfish for me? And I do believe you're the best friend I've ever had! But haven't you realised yet that I love you, too?'

His throat moved convulsively. 'You love me?'

'So very much, my darling, so very much!' Her eyes glowed with emotion as she gazed up at him adoringly. 'Admittedly you can be arrogant and bossy, and you're incredibly single-minded...'

'But...?' He laughed shakily as she listed his faults.

'But I love you anyway,' she assured him with an incandescent smile. 'Drakon, do you remember I once told you that I've felt incomplete all my life?' she said. 'As if a part of me were missing?'

'Because you lost your twin.'

'You complete me, Drakon. Totally and utterly,' Gemini told him fervently.

Drakon took a deep breath. 'And I am so consumed with love for you I don't know how I ever existed without you.'

'I feel exactly the same way,' Gemini vowed, before Drakon's lips claimed hers and there was no more talk from either of them for a considerable amount of time.

'We must stop now, my darling.' Drakon drew back reluctantly in one of the armchairs, Gemini nestled comfortably in his arms. 'I have waited this long to make love with you. I can wait a little longer,' he insisted as she looked up at him in silent reproach. 'But first—will you marry me, Gemini?'

Her eyes widened. 'Marriage, Drakon? Are you sure?'

'Totally and utterly.' He firmly repeated her words of earlier. 'I love you to distraction. I had no idea what loneliness was until I was faced with the thought of never seeing you again, never being with you again.' His arms tightened about her. 'Will you marry me and complete me also, Gemini?'

'Oh, yes, Drakon, I'll marry you,' she accepted, before throwing her arms about his neck and kissing him enthusiastically. 'But where will we live?' She sobered. 'At the moment your business and home is in New York, and I live and work here in London.'

Drakon smiled. 'I am sure that Markos will not mind moving to New York in my place. I will transfer to the offices here, to London.'

Gemini's eyes were wide. 'You would do that for me?'

'My love, have you not realised yet that I would do and be anything for you?' He gazed down at her with those intense dark eyes.

Oh, yes, Gemini knew exactly what lengths Drakon was willing to go to in order to ensure her happiness. 'Then perhaps it's time I made some sort of sacrifice for you?' she said.

'In this instance it is not necessary that you do so,' he replied. 'Besides, would you not prefer that our children grow up in Bartholomew House?'

Drakon's children. And hers… Gemini had thought she couldn't possibly be any happier than she was, but the thought of having Drakon's children made her feel full to bursting.

'Do you regret having to give up Bartholomew House?'

He shrugged. 'To Lyonedes Enterprises it was only ever a piece of real estate, but to you it was always so much more. We will find somewhere else in London to build our hotel. Besides,' Drakon added teasingly, 'I haven't given up anything; Bartholomew House now belongs to my future wife and the mother of my children.'

It was truly unbelievable that she could be this happy.

'In that case, I would like it very much if you moved to London,' she breathed softly.

His arms tightened about her. 'Then it shall be so. And tomorrow we will go out and buy an indecently expensive engagement ring— No?' he said, when he saw the uncertainty in her face.

'I—would you mind very much if we used my mother's engagement ring instead?' Gemini looked up at him anxiously.

Drakon smiled down at her indulgently. 'You do not wish for a new and indecently expensive ring?'

She smiled ruefully as she shook her head. 'We can have new matching wedding bands. But if you don't mind I would really like to wear my mother's engagement ring.'

Drakon reached down and picked up the box from where it had fallen when they'd begun to kiss each other, flicking open the lid and taking out the emerald and diamond ring.

'I will love you for eternity, Gemini,' he pledged as he slipped the ring onto her finger.

'As I will love you, Drakon,' she vowed in return.

Two weeks later, on their wedding night, Drakon carried Gemini into the master bedroom of his house on the island in the Aegean Sea, pushing aside the gauzy curtains around a four-poster bed surrounded by the perfume of dozens upon dozens of rose petals. They lay down upon the covers and made long and beautiful love with each other...

* * * * *

MODERN™

INTERNATIONAL AFFAIRS, SEDUCTION & PASSION GUARANTEED

My wish list for next month's titles...

In stores from 18th May 2012:

☐ A Secret Disgrace – Penny Jordan

☐ The Forbidden Ferrara – Sarah Morgan

☐ Enemies at the Altar – Melanie Milburne

☐ In Defiance of Duty – Caitlin Crews

In stores from 1st June 2012:

☐ The Dark Side of Desire – Julia James

☐ The Truth Behind his Touch – Cathy Williams

☐ A World She Doesn't Belong To – Natasha Tate

☐ In the Italian's Sights – Helen Brooks

☐ Dare She Kiss & Tell? – Aimee Carson

Available at WHSmith, Tesco, Asda, Eason, Amazon and Apple

Just can't wait?

2 Free Books!

Get your free books now at
www.millsandboon.co.uk/freebookoffer

Or fill in the form below and post it back to us

Mrs/Miss/Ms/Mr (please circle)

First Name

Surname

Address

Postcode

Email

Send this completed page to: Mills & Boon Book Club, Free Book Offer, FREEPOST NAT 10298, Richmond, Surrey, TW9 1BR

Find out more at
www.millsandboon.co.uk/freebookoffer

Visit us Online

0112/P2XEA/REV